Devin's Best Afterlife

The Current Mr. Orr, Volume 1

Sean Boling

Published by Sean Boling, 2022.

This is a work of fiction. Similarities to real people, places, or events are entirely coincidental.

DEVIN'S BEST AFTERLIFE

First edition. January 5, 2022.

ISBN: 979-8224211517

Written by Sean Boling.

Chapter One

The launch is smooth. Every glitch was fixed during crunch. I watch the demonstration play out on the cinema-sized screen from backstage, and still hold my breath whenever the professional gamer we hired to play in front of the thousands in attendance and hundreds of thousands online reaches an old problem spot.

The part after the cutscene when Tara leaves Mitch to seek her own fortune and she finds the cache of weapons.

The beginning of the battle in the desert when the Replicators rise from underneath the sand.

Half the time the player switches from third person to first person perspective.

Every time Tara reaches for the laser lasso.

"We should have recorded the demo," I say out loud at one point.

One of my assistants, Kelly, reminds me that live is better.

"Especially at a live event."

She does not have to remind me. I was not talking to anyone in particular, least of all her and her jokes. Not all of her jokes are bad. Some are pretty good, but there are too many of them. I have been hoping for months she will post something she thinks is funny on one of her social media accounts that winds up offensive and viral so I can fire her. I would prefer Jalen or Gina by my side, but they are too valuable to fill the sidekick gig. I need them circulating around the venue, overseeing the logistics.

I look upward at all the lights and tug at the quarter-zip pullover I chose to wear, wondering if I should take it off. It may be too hot, but the dress shirt underneath may reveal some perspiration, so I would need to wear one of blazers hanging on the rack behind me, which puts me right back to being too hot. The pullover adds the right amount of casual to my look. Plus if I take it off, someone will have to fix my hair. I should be doing relaxation exercises, not fretting over my wardrobe.

When it is almost time for my speech, Kelly reminds me that it is almost time for my speech.

"When the announcer introduces me," I sigh, "are you going to tell me that's my cue?"

"I might."

She is overbearing, but willing to be teased about it.

The announcer introduces me.

She takes a deep breath as if to say something, catches herself on purpose, and smiles.

I smile back with a small laugh and decide if that offensive tweet ever lands, I will let her off with a warning.

My speech is on point. Everything disappears but the words in my head. Every word offers itself to me, and each one feels important. Even the conjunctions and articles of speech have value. *But, or, and, so, the, an, a*...they are not small words, they are connections and setups for big ideas. I do not need the teleprompter. I have given the speech before, but this time is different, as if my whole life has led up to this few minutes, like an Olympic athlete, a gymnast or swimmer, who spends almost all of the points on their timeline to prepare for a single point. The theme of my speech has been used before by many game developers, the one about how video games are like life, but with second chances...and third chances, and fourth, fifth, sixth. That line earns some laughs. But the earnest moments are what sells it. The best is when I elaborate on what I mean by "chances", defining them as opportunities to fix a mistake, to right a wrong, all of those things we wish we could do in real life, but rarely can. This is what we want most from games, the parts that are the least like life.

I want to take a deep, long bow when I am done, but that would undermine the veneer of sincerity I have reached, so I nod my head. The audience seems to agree that it went well. They do more than applaud, they cheer. I look forward to the question and answer session, more so than any before. I look backstage for more validation.

Kelly gestures for me to join her. I rear back. Not a chance. I want to keep the momentum going. I ignore her and look out at the audience.

Jalen stands in front of the first row, gesturing me to go backstage.

Gina walks down the aisle on the right, giving me the same signal.

I grimace in frustration, camouflaging it with a big wave to the crowd, hoping to make it look like a smile. As I exit the stage, I point to various people who look particularly excited and make eye contact with them, laying the foundation for an encore once I get to the bottom of what is going on backstage.

Kelly is not waiting for me. She is walking away, beckoning me to follow.

"What?" I demand as I shadow her.

She says nothing, leading me deeper into the recesses of the venue. We take some turns around some curtains, pass behind the screen, take more turns around more curtains, and meet up with Jalen and Gina.

"What on earth?" I try them, but they are just as unresponsive.

Jalen is holding open a curtain. Gina gestures for me to enter the opening.

Kelly falls back.

"Please, sir," she says from behind me.

"I need to get back out there," I say.

"That's what this is about," says Gina.

"A trap door?" I ask. "I can come up through the floor? Slowly rise for my encore? Great idea."

"You'll see," says Jalen.

"Fine," I brush off their severity. "Oh, wait. I get it. A surprise party."

I move toward the open curtain.

"You're overselling the misdirection," I tease them. "The launch went perfectly. The demo, the speech, all of it. This dramatic routine you worked out doesn't fit."

I enter the space created by curtains and find myself staring back at me.

I do not mean I am looking inward. I am not using figurative language when I say I am looking at myself. There is an actual me, a person who looks exactly like me and is dressed like me, standing in front of me.

"Surprise!" he says.

All I can do is stare at him.

I hear Kelly ask, "Is this really necessary?"

"I was curious," the he who is me says. "I wanted to see how it would react."

"It?" I break my silence, still staring.

My twin stares back, but his look is calm and probing, while I imagine mine is stunned and bewildered.

I hear Gina ask, "Should we tell him?"

The other me closes the book on his study of my expression.

"I need to get back out there," he says. "Just stick to the plan."

Jalen grabs me from behind.

I feel a poke in my neck before I can put up a struggle.

Gina appears in front of me, holding a syringe.

"I'm sorry," she says.

"Let's go," the other me commands.

Kelly joins him. She looks back at me and seems to want to add to Gina's apology.

My body is numb. Jalen releases me and I collapse.

He straightens me out on the floor and positions himself above my head. Gina stands below my feet. They reach down to lift me up.

"Hold on," Gina says.

"The truck is waiting," Jalen reminds her.

"I didn't think he'd last this long," she walks over by my side. "Give me ten seconds to tell him what's going on."

"Ten seconds?" I want to say, but cannot speak. "You can explain this in ten seconds?"

"I don't think that's a good idea," Jalen warns her.

"Devin insisting on revealing himself like some hack magician off the Vegas strip was a bad idea," Gina quips. "This is damage control."

"Fine," Jalen shrugs. "What's ten seconds?"

"Took the words right out of my mouth," I imagine saying.

Gina kneels down next to me.

"You're a clone," she says. "You were created by Devin to make public appearances while he worked crunch time. He worked on the game remotely, so no one knew there was a double. He had you handle the launch today in case it didn't go well."

If I could speak, it would not matter. I would still be speechless.

"Feel better?" Jalen teases her.

"Feel anything?" Gina fires back.

Their bickering continues as I lose consciousness, if I ever really was conscious.

Chapter Two

I am in an office, in a cubicle, in a chair next to an empty desk.

The chair in front of the desk is empty. I am a guest, or a client.

It sounds like a large office. There is a throb of humming machines, ring tones, and conversations. I stand up and look over the barriers. I am in one out of a hundred cubicles. Dozens of heads glide along the tops of the other barriers. I look for a logo, a company name on one of the walls, but they are all blank.

"Mr. Orr," a voice says my name.

I turn around to find a man who matches the surroundings.

"Thank you for waiting," he says. "Please have a seat."

I comply.

"We won't keep you long. I'm sure you're eager to get started. We just like to cover a thing or two before you head out into this new phase."

He sits down in his chair.

"Before you...level up," he makes sure I get the joke about what I do for a living.

I ignore it.

"Boot up?" he fishes for the right reference.

"Where am I?"

His face slackens, and the droop has nothing to do with me not appreciating his sense of humor.

"You don't know?"

I shake my head.

"No dead relative told you?"

"What?"

"There's always a dead parent or grandparent, dead father figure or mother figure. They show up and tell you to walk into the light, or avoid the pit, something symbolic. They guide you. Sometimes they throw in a profound thought, or a totally baffling one."

The word "baffling" resonates with me. I know I am staring and my mouth is probably hanging open, but I am way beyond worrying about appearances.

"No?" he asks. "None of that?"

"Nobody told me anything."

He exhales and leans back in his chair.

"Is there a problem?" I ask.

"I've never had to break the news to anyone," he slumps forward and puts his head in his hands. "I just run through the orientation."

"Is this...?"

He groans and runs his hands down his face, then holds them up in my direction, as if I have a gun I am threatening to use.

"Before you got here," he enunciates. "Do you remember anything about those last moments? Anything anyone said or did?"

"I certainly do."

He brightens up.

"Really?"

"I met an exact double of myself, then my assistants ganged up on me and injected me with some kind of drug, and one of them told me I'm a clone who was created so that I could be in two places at once. Or that he could be. We could be. I'm trying to come up with a sentence that doesn't admit he's the original and I'm the copy."

His brightness fades. The droop returns.

"So am I dead?" I ask. "Or am I tripping on that drug they gave me?"

He looks at me, long enough to be uncomfortable if he was really looking at me, but he has a lot on his mind and I happen to be sitting in his line of sight.

He slides his chair away from the desk.

"Will you excuse me for a moment?" he rises and wanders out of the cubicle.

I stand and watch his head make its way through the maze of temporary little walls until he reaches an office with a window in the permanent wall at the end of his route. He taps on the door, walks in, and talks to someone who is sitting down, out of view. Soon the man he is talking to stands up, and both of them exit. Their heads float toward me on the sea of cubicles. I sit down and wait for their arrival.

The distraught man whose cubicle I am sitting in enters first and introduces the man who follows.

"Mr. Orr, this is my manager."

I rise and shake his hand.

"Do you have a name?" I ask.

His grip is firm.

"I have a problem," he says.

"Use my chair," his underling offers. "I'll go find another one."

The manager obliges and sits at the desk of the underling, who darts back out to find that other chair. I sit back down in mine.

"It seems clone technology is one step ahead of us," the manager settles in for a conversation. "Maybe more."

"You believe me then."

"It explains a lot."

He reaches for a tablet on the desk, pulls it toward him, and taps the screen.

"It would explain why people have made appointments to see you, including some dead relatives, but none of them greeted you during the crossover."

"Appointments?" I ask.

The underling rolls a chair through the opening.

"Residents are required to make them with arrivals," he blurts while catching his breath.

He parks the chair beside his manager.

"Sorry," he sits. "That's part of the orientation. My spiel. I feel like I haven't been very helpful so far."

"You called our attention to this problem," the manager credits him.

The underling continues, bolstered by his manager's approval.

"We can't assume arrivals are going to want to see everyone they know here. This is meant to be a custom-made experience, and having to deal with someone you never really liked before can ruin that. Death can make unpleasant people more sympathetic or likeable to the living, but over here, you still have to deal with them."

"Most residents understand that," the manager adds. "Requesting an appointment and being denied is embarrassing. If they know they weren't on the best terms with a new arrival, they'll pass."

"And I have some requests?"

The manager and underling look at each other.

"Which brings us back to the problem," the manager takes charge.

We all nod in recognition of the problem, and keep nodding as we realize something.

"What exactly is the problem?" I ask.

"Well..."

"Hmm..."

"It's not that you're a clone, per se," the manager works through a definition out loud. "It's that you're a clone who made it this far."

"Thank you for saying 'who.'"

"Well, you're enough of a who to send out a signal."

"A signal?"

"The thing that alerts the others you're on your way," the underling jumps in. "You have to be human to do that."

"Or just human enough," the manager seems to be talking to himself as much as to me. "It's funny how the residents got the message to make appointments with you, but nobody greeted you during the transition. I guess the signal was delayed."

"Better than the other way around," I suppose. "That would kind of suck to be greeted, then have no appointments when I got here."

"You're also fairly young," he keeps chasing an answer. "Well, Devin Orr is fairly young. You're extremely young. What, a few months old?"

"Maybe," I shrug. "If I had known I was what I am, I could tell you."

"How many requests does Mr. Orr have?" he turns to the underling, who rolls over to nab his tablet from the desk and consult the screen.

"Four."

"Four?" I parrot him. "That sounds low. Is that low?"

"It's not high," the underling hedges.

"Younger people always have lower numbers," the manager says. "Who put in the requests?"

"A grandfather," the underling says more to him than to me, "a great-aunt, someone named Jane Lamar, and someone named Phil Dedmon."

"Dedmon?" the manager notes.

The underling spells it for him.

"Still," says the manager. "What a coincidence."

"That's not our first Dedmon."

"Exactly."

The underling stares at the manager, who stares back, neither sure if the other is joking.

I feel a chilling jolt of adrenalin unrelated to their staring contest.

"Is it possible to turn down a request?" I ask.

They go from staring to looking at each other.

"Yes," the manager proceeds with caution. "If you didn't harm the person making the request."

"Arrivals cannot avoid their victims," the underling explains.

"Are any of those names flagged as a victim of something Mr. Orr did?" the manager asks his subordinate.

"No," the underling replies before double-checking the screen. "No."

"Which one are you thinking of denying?" the manager asks me.

"I'm thinking the great-aunt," I say. "I have this feeling, like the anxiety going on right now between us, this is what it's like to be around her."

"Really..." the manager leans in.

"I couldn't describe her, I'm not sure I'd know her if I saw her, but I think that's how my mind works, how it connects with Devin's."

"Emotional triggers," he encourages me to continue as the underling looks on.

"When I would be at an event, raising money, promoting the game, talking to people," I build on my realization, "I could tell stories from my past, from his past, if somebody said or did something that reminded me of a memory that fit the moment. Like if you asked me if I've ever been skiing, I would know if he did and could answer the question, but if you asked me to tell a funny story about one time when I was skiing, I wouldn't be able to do it. I would find a way to ignore the question or make something up. I need to feel something to recall a memory. The smell of pine trees might lead to one of those skiing stories. Or if I pull a muscle and the same thing happened on the slopes one time, that would bring back a memory."

"Which is the same as creating one in your case," the manager studies me. "They programmed you to build memories rather than load them all at once. Interesting."

"Sounds like I'm not your first clone."

"The keynote speaker at one of the conferences I had to attend for my job talked about entrance screening. She said we've been able to spot Artificial intelligence pretty easily so far because we can tell it's artificial. Since a lot of your memories arrive more, I don't know, organically? That might be what crossed us up."

"I thought this job was so routine," the underling muses.

His manager glares at him.

"This is interesting," the underling explains. "I was getting into a rut."

"What about the other residents who requested an appointment," the manager guides us back to the situation at hand. "Any feelings about them?"

"Nothing major. The grandfather used to sing a goofy little song to me, to Devin. The other two, no connections at all. Maybe they're tech fans who want to meet me."

"We don't allow that," the underling seizes the chance to come across as more professional. "Think of the really famous people who arrive. We can't drop millions of requests in their lap. The signal only goes out to residents who have some kind of personal relationship to you."

"And what then? Are these appointments in the true sense of the word? I sit in an office or a café and meet with them, like a job interview?"

"They appear at some point," the underling keeps up his momentum as the manager sinks deeper into thought. "You build your world, imagine the places where you want to hang out, things you want to do, and they show up eventually depending on how they fit into the situations."

"If this is a custom-made experience," I allow myself to dive into the world that might be waiting for me, "what about people who aren't here yet that you would like to spend time with?"

"You can make projections of them. Place holders until the real deals get here."

"Clones," I quip.

The underling wobbles in search of a comeback.

"They're not nearly as sophisticated," the manager comes to his rescue. "Even the clones that came before you are way beyond the projections that are created here. The projections only function in the presence of the resident who conjures them up."

"Us clones have agency," I say. "We have autonomy."

"That's right."

The more I learn, the more I want to stay and grow.

"So maybe my being here isn't really a problem."

"You still emerged from another life."

"Don't we all?" I spread my arms. "Well, maybe not you guys. Are you human? Something else? What, precisely?"

"We work here," the manager maintains.

"Anyone higher up I can speak to?" I grin at the possibilities of who or what might be in upper management.

"I'll fill them in after we've had a chance to hash things out here."

I am intrigued by the pronoun *them*.

"Who are they?"

"Those who have worked their way up."

"Are they like you?"

"How so?"

"Nameless, faceless drones."

The manager gathers himself while the underling pretends to study his screen.

"Mr. Orr," the manager proceeds. "I understand that learning about your circumstances so suddenly before they ended must be difficult. But who you are, what you are, is not our fault."

"Of course not," I backtrack. "You'll have to excuse me. I have a feeling the person I'm based on is not a very nice person."

"That excuse is going to come in so handy," the underling mutters.

"That excuse is not going to be necessary," the manager addresses him while looking at me. "If this version of Mr. Orr is allowed entrance, he needs to keep playing the role of Mr. Orr, as his creator intended."

"I take it they don't provide you with sensitivity training here," I meet his gaze.

"Ugh," the underling groans. "They most certainly do."

"No kidding?" I am shocked to have my snark revealed as fact. "I'll bet that gets really wild. You've got way more than race and gender going on. What did you say you were again?"

"We are not your concern," the manager remains steadfast. "You are our concern."

"Am I that big of a concern, though? My list is so small. I've whittled it down from four to three."

"Think of the confusion when the real Devin arrives."

"I'll cross them all off. I won't meet anyone. I'll do my own thing."

"The signal has already been sent."

"So you're stuck with me."

The manager retreats back into thinking out loud.

"Maybe we can claim it was a false alarm."

"There you go," I encourage him.

"That only takes care of the current circumstances," he returns to addressing me. "More people who know him are going to arrive as time passes. You might bump into them."

"From what we've been discussing, it sounds like I'll probably get the signals. If that's the case, I won't request any appointments."

"We don't know if that's going to be the case."

"Then I'll keep an eye on Devin, see who he's hanging out with, and avoid them when they make the jump."

"We don't allow that either," the underling once again swoops on an opportunity to go over the rules. "No eavesdropping on the living. Residents looking in on earth might start longing for their past, when they need to be focusing on building their new life."

"People love to imagine the dead looking down on them," I ponder this latest revelation. "I heard them say it more than once, and I was only there for who knows how many weeks or months."

"Which is fine for them," the manager contends. "But not healthy for the people here. The dead need to move on."

"What about ghosts?"

"Residents find a way to break through now and then, usually by accident. We find out pretty quickly and fix the leak. Sometimes a small part of them gets left behind when we pull them back. Very small, more like a tiny part, which is why ghosts tend to have that one thing they do, in one place, sporadically."

I think of my limited purpose for existing.

"How far can you go to stop me from going in?"

"Not very far," the manager admits.

"Our job is about making lives, not taking lives," the underling falls back on reciting the rule book.

"Catchy."

"It's part of the orientation."

I figured, but try to look surprised.

The manager offers a less glossy spin.

"Ending you would kind of undermine the mission statement."

"But you don't want me here."

The manager runs through a series of small contortions in his chair.

"Honestly?" he says. "I don't think establishing residency is a good idea."

"Fair enough," I concede. "So what exactly can you do to keep me out?"

"Two things," he glances at the underling to see if he wants to quote the options chapter and verse, hoping that he will.

"I know what they are," the underling shrinks. "But I never include them in my slide show. Going stardust has its own department, and nobody worries about that until they've been here long enough to forget I ever mentioned it, and mulligans are handled before any of them get to me."

"Going stardust?" I pry. "Mulligans?"

The manager has no choice.

"Those are slang terms," he drags himself into the lead. "We've used them so long none of us really know what the official names are, if they have names. As you may have already noticed, a lot of things don't have names or titles here. They just are."

"And what is it that these things 'just are'?"

"Going stardust is when a resident has grown tired of the world they've created here. They put in a request, and once it's approved, they can go through a door, through a curtain, whatever they decide, and they don't come out the other side. One guy did a cliff dive into the ocean."

"That was awesome," the underling recalls.

"What happens to them?"

"Like the term implies, they vanish, turn to stardust, join the elements of the universe. We don't know for sure."

"How could anyone grow tired of doing whatever they want?"

The manager and underling look at each other and try not to scoff before looking back my way.

"You really are young," the manager says.

"To be fair," the underling comes to my defense. "Most people take forever to get tired of it."

"Some don't take long at all," the manager adds.

He would like me to get there now.

"And a mulligan?" I change the subject.

"Not as straightforward as it sounds," the underling says.

He waits for the manager to bounce off the setup he provided, but the manager remains mute. The underling almost looks at him, but stops short and obeys the quiet command.

"It's a do-over, but not the same life," he explains. "It's a fresh body, newly born, randomly chosen, and the person remembers nothing that came before. It's reserved for people who didn't have a chance to experience enough about the world to create their version of it here."

"Children," I assume.

"Mostly," he confirms. "Some adults need a mulligan, thanks to cognitive disabilities."

"And you call it a mulligan?"

"Not ideal," he concedes.

"Nobody on earth knows what we call it," the manager brushes past the concern.

"So you guys play golf over here?"

"We've heard of it," he pushes for an end to the semantics discussion.

The underling helps him get there.

"Every so often I'll have a child who makes it to orientation," he shares an exception. "Since they lived a rich enough life to give them plenty to work with here. Or I meet an adult who was homebound or unable to communicate but had a vivid imagination."

I sit in my adult body with the lived experiences of a child and begin to speculate on the variety of lives that a random choice could land on, the likeliness of poverty and struggle, the long odds of comfort and prosperity.

"I don't imagine I can convince you to go stardust," the manager cuts back in.

I am still constructing my Mulligan Probability Model.

"But a mulligan may be possible," he says.

"May be?"

"Your case needs to be evaluated, which I suspect will take a while, given that we've never seen anything like you before, and committees being what they are."

"A committee?"

"Yes."

"My case is going before a committee?"

"It's a big universe, Mr. Orr. We're a team."

His words and the feelings they inspire make me think of all the jobs Devin has had, the ones I have access to. All of them insisted their employees use the pronoun "we" when referring to the company, no matter the level of employee satisfaction or turnover rate. I wonder if this office of the dead I am sitting in has been designed to provide new residents a sense of familiarity, or if workplaces of the living have evolved to look like this office due to a slowly evolving awareness of what lies beyond.

"In the meantime what do I do?" I ask. "Hang out here in the office? Order takeout? Is there a couch I can sleep on?"

He starts to answer me, fails to progress beyond an opening syllable, then grabs the underling by the arm.

"Will you excuse us?" he says while guiding him out of the cubicle.

They walk far enough away so that I can hear their voices but not the words they form. The tone is heated and the pace rapid. Neither sounds like the one in charge.

The hushed intensity comes to an abrupt stop and seconds later, the underling returns to the cubicle by himself.

"We decided it was time to bring this to the attention of our administrators," he announces while standing in the opening. "He's on his way up there now."

"Okay."

He continues to stand for a moment, then pushes the spare chair aside and sits back down at his desk in his original chair.

We sit in silence for another moment before he looks for a task to pantomime.

I stare straight ahead to avoid making him uncomfortable. I think about what happened backstage at the launch maybe fifteen minutes ago, depending on how time works between these two places, and wonder if another surprise is coming.

"Actually," he says at low volume, "we do have names."

"Excuse me?" I fail to follow his lead on the volume.

"Those of us who work here," he sticks with his near-whisper. "We have given ourselves names. Some of us."

"Oh."

I figure if he wants to tell me his name, he will.

"Mine is Melt," he confides.

"Did you say 'Melt'?"

"Yes," he stifles a laugh.

I almost ask him to tell me the story, but again do not need to ask.

"I was giving an orientation to a really nice woman from southern Mexico," he tells me. "Her nickname was Mely. I liked her, I liked her name, and thought it was about time I had a name, so I named myself after her. But when I used it for the first time in a message I sent to a colleague, I accidentally typed the letter 't' at the end instead of a 'y' when I signed off. They're right next to each other on the keyboard. Melt. I explained to my colleague what happened, but it was too late. It stuck."

"You speak Spanish?"

"Mely didn't speak Spanish. She was indigenous."

"So you speak her native language?"

"Whatever language someone speaks, that's what I use for their orientation."

He returns his attention to his desk and appears to discover a legitimate task he really needs to do.

I watch him and try to reconcile his knowledge of every language on earth with his being an anxious office ninny.

"Huh," I grunt in wonder.

I sit back and listen to the hum of the surrounding workplace. If someone in his position has such a knack, all the working stiffs within earshot must have a similar, if not greater, connection to the universe. I workshop some ideas on why it would be advantageous for a lifeform so advanced to evolve such a remedial husk. Camouflage? Comfort? Accommodation?

"So in all these other languages," I hear myself say, "do you still call it a mulligan?"

He stops working on his task and wonders where to begin.

The manager returns and spares him from having to.

"Some news," the manager proclaims from the cubicle gap.

"Good news or bad news?" I ask.

"That's not for me to say."

"Unbiased reporting. I suppose I should appreciate that."

"Administration has decided you can stay while they deliberate your case and come to a decision."

The underling smiles at me as if to encourage me to do the same.

"Stay," I say. "Stay here? In the office?"

"No," the manager sounds too relieved and overcorrects himself. "No. Not here in the office. Here as a resident. They want you to continue being Devin. And they mean it when they say 'be Devin'. Play along with anyone from his life you encounter."

"That should be easy," the underling clings to the bright side. "You were made for that."

"If you refuse appointments it might look suspicious," the manager expands. "They need you to buy some time while they figure out how much of a ripple this may have caused, and how to tackle whatever that ripple may have rocked."

"Any idea how long that could be?"

"They don't care for self-imposed deadlines," the manager explains. "They prefer to let things play out as they must."

I piece together the criticism I want to deliver.

"Explain to me," I slowly release it, "how all of you can speak every language in the universe, how you can manage who knows how many simulations of people's lives that, combined, might be bigger than the universe it simulates, and how you can do who knows what else you know how to do, but you can't make a decision any faster than the average committee of human beings who hate being on the committee."

"Those skills of ours," the manager is ready with his response, "those are all tools, crafts we have learned. Making a decision is something completely different. Especially one concerning a brand new problem."

"Brand new," I like the way that phrase makes my problem sound.

The manager smiles. He gestures for the underling to hand him the tablet on his desk. The underling obeys, and the manager taps on it.

"Look at this," he holds it up so I can see the screen. "This is a time-lapse video of the area where you spent most of your time on earth. It covers a thousand years per second."

I watch clouds and stars rocket through the sky that blinks black and blue, the moon sways back and forth, trees rise and fall, waters rise and subside, indiscernible objects appear and disappear, lights flash.

"Do you see yourself anywhere in there?" he asks me.

"Of course not."

"That's right," he wipes away the video and hands the tablet back to the underling. "Of course not."

"You've used that before," I suppose.

"People can sometimes feel a little too special when they discover they can create their own world."

"People," I shake my head and commiserate.

"Play along with them," he reminds me.

"How do I get where I need to be?"

The underling is back on the job.

"Think of a place where you liked spending time," he settles into his routine. "That's the best way to start. Nothing fancy. Don't try anywhere you've never been before. Choose someplace familiar, comfortable."

He sounds like he is trying to conduct a relaxation exercise, or hypnotize me. It does not suit him. He is the farthest thing from a soothing presence. But he can speak any language in the world, in the universe, so I go with it.

Chapter Three

I am in a coffee house. The team and I went to a lot of them in the lead-up to the launch. This is one of the nicer ones, the kind with exposed brick and beams. I have never been to Devin's house, and have only a vague notion of what it looks like. I stayed in hotels during crunch, my time on earth. They were nice hotels, but when I think of them, I feel lonely, so I went with the high-end coffee house. We met a small group of tech journalists here to discuss the game. None of them are here now, they are all still alive. Maybe some of the projections that are sitting at other tables or standing in line are based on them, or other people who were here that day, but my memories of them are too fleeting and buried to identify anyone.

I am already seated with a porcelain cup of Americano I can't remember ordering, but I know it has three shots of espresso, the way Devin likes it. I wonder if I can develop tastes of my own. I vow to place new orders during my stay. If I think of a restaurant and am suddenly sitting there with a seared ahi tuna burger already in front of me, I will send it back and ask to see the menu.

"Shooter!" a voice bellows.

I flinch and make a move to get under the table but see that nobody else is concerned.

"Shooter," the older man repeats himself at a lower volume.

He approaches my table, arms outstretched.

"Relax, kiddo. It's just me. Great to see you!"

"Great to see you, too…" I realize who it is, "Grandpa."

I stand up and accept his hug. He does not look as old as I expected.

"I haven't heard that name in a while," I say over the macho back slaps that accompany our embrace.

"Oh," he stands back and keeps his hands on my shoulders. "Is that why you…?"

He nods at the table and makes a mock scared face.

"That is why," I confess.

He bursts out laughing, his hands leaving my shoulders to keep from busting a gut.

"What a coincidence," he gasps.

"How so?"

"Well," he catches his breath. "I never told you the real reason I called you that."

"Oh," I remember the apparently fake reason and am excited that it came to me. "It's not from shooting baskets in your driveway?"

"The hoop wasn't in the driveway," he takes offense. "We had a basketball court in the back, by the putting green."

"Ah," I am disappointed in how many details the memory is missing.

"You don't remember?"

"Sorry," I mean it, but not for any setbacks to his ego. "Just died. Still adapting."

"That's okay," he tries to convince himself. "You probably didn't have a lot of pleasant memories on that court."

"I wasn't much of a player."

"You were ridiculous," he regains his laughter.

"But that's not why you called me Shooter."

"Nope," he settles down to set up his revelation. "I thought you were gonna be a school shooter."

"What?"

He releases more jolly noise.

"That's not funny," I scold.

"What's the big deal?" he waves away my concern. "Look at you now."

"Dead."

"Before that. You still had your company, right?"

"Yes."

"A big shot tech guy."

He realizes how well the term applies to his unveiling of the wicked nickname.

"Big shot!" he repeats it.

"Would you like to order something?" I move us along.

"Nah, I'm okay. I don't care for these kinds of places. Gimme a donut shop any day."

"A real man of the people," I sit down and gesture for him to do likewise. "Have a seat at least."

I watch him settle into the chair with ease.

"You're not as old as I thought you'd be, Grandpa."

"I'm even younger in my usual hangout spots."

"Really?"

"Why would anyone build a world and make themselves an old fart?"

"That's a fair question."

"I went a little older for this joint so you'd recognize me."

"Thank you."

"Plus it would be pretty freaky to have your grandpa be younger than you."

"Probably."

"So..." he rocks in his chair. "You know, maybe I will have something."

"They have donuts."

"Yeah?"

"Good ones. Artisan donuts."

"Ha! Well, all right then."

He gets up and walks to the counter to place his order. I wonder what he wants to say that is making him ill at ease. I sip my coffee and wait.

"Mmm," he takes a bite as he sits back down. "That is good."

"So how is the afterlife treating you?" I ask.

"Beautiful. What's not to love?"

I think of how different my experience has been so far, the office workers and management team and committees, which keeps me quiet, which prompts him to get to what is bothering him.

"How's your grandmother?" he asks.

"I didn't see much of her," I say, which I suspect is true enough for Devin. I never met her in my role, and no connections are emerging.

"Did you hear much? Is she healthy?"

"You miss her, huh?"

He picks at his donut.

"She'll be here soon enough," I assure him. "And when she does get here, you'll have an eternity together if you want it."

He looks out the window.

"Nice work," he motions toward the cityscape outside and pops a piece of donut into his mouth.

"I didn't think much about it. Not sure where all that came from."

"Hmm," he nods and after some time finally swallows the bite.

I know next to nothing about him, or his wife. He may as well be a troubled stranger at the next table, visibly upset enough to prompt a fellow stranger to reach out, only I happen to have one piece of information I can use to ask something other than what is wrong.

"Do you remember the song you used to sing me?" I ask.

He smiles.

"Boop boop dittem dattem wattem chu," he sings.

I join him.

"Boop boop dittem dattem wattem chu," we both sing.

We let it rip for the final line.

"And they swam and they swam all over the dam!"

Some of the customers looks at us and smile. I acknowledge them, and look at Devin's grandfather, but he is no longer smiling.

"Did I ever mention the name Angela Van Earle to you?" he asks.

"No."

"Of course not," he admonishes himself. "Why would I? You were so young when we used to spend time with you. The older you got, the less we saw you."

"By 'we' you mean you and grandma, not this Angela..." I reach for the name.

"Van Earle," he hands it to me.

"And what would you have told me about Angela Van Earle if we had spent more time together when I was older and you mentioned her?"

I feel a little more like his grandson, but even more like his priest.

"She's somebody I knew before I met your grandmother."

Now I am the one laughing.

"I thought you'd be upset," he seems disappointed.

"It's your afterlife," I submit. "Is she a projection? Or the real deal? Whatever that means around here."

"She's the real deal, all right."

"I'll bet she looks really young too."

"Oh, boy. Does she. Wanna see a picture?"

He reaches into his pocket.

"No," I hold up my hand. "Thank you. Not interested."

"Okay," his hand retreats from his pocket. "I get it. Look, I love your grandmother. I'd like to see her when she arrives. But I've been saying things to Angela. Overdoing it."

"Should be easy enough to juggle two women here. I'm sure there's lots you can do with space and time."

"I told Angela I never should have let her go back in the day, that she's the true love of my life. And to prove it, I told her I'd go stardust when your grandmother gets here."

I could laugh, but I am too fascinated.

He is too panicked to notice my reaction either way.

"Going stardust is forever, Shooter. Uh, Devin."

"I'm fresh off my orientation," I remind him. "I know."

"There's nothing after that. Nothing!"

"So you don't really love Angela that much?"

He leans from side to side.

"She's a fantastic lay..." he considers how much that counts.

"Just not cast-yourself-into-the-void fantastic," I presume.

He leans back and covers his face with his hands.

"It felt so good to think with my dick again," he moans through his fingers. "I hadn't been able to do that for so long."

"An eternity?"

He releases his face and lurches forward.

"I have a plan."

"I would love to hear it."

And I mean that.

Devin's grandfather leans in to avoid the universe eavesdropping.

"I'm gonna fake going stardust."

"Nothing to it," I deadpan.

"I'm not trying to put one over on the management, or administration. I'm not stupid. I just need to fake out Angela."

"So what's your not-stupid plan?"

"A magic trick."

I sip from my porcelain cup of Americano to see if I can complete the action without spewing out a spit take.

"It's my world, after all," he explains. "I can learn to be a good magician."

"So..." I imagine how this might play out. "You're going to go through a door that you claim is your stardust portal, and then have a trap door on the other side. Something like that?"

"Hmm," he looks impressed. "I hadn't thought of that. I was thinking of using one of those big down comforters. We have one on our bed. They offer a lot of wiggle room, and they're really lumpy, so I can move around under it easily."

"All good reasons."

"See, I want to pull off my vanishing act right after doing it one last time."

If he really was my grandfather, this is when I would excuse myself to use the bathroom. Instead, I grow more intrigued.

"Why are you telling me all this?" I ask him.

"What do you mean? You're my grandson."

"I would think a grandfather would want to keep this from his grandson."

"It's a chance to bond. To be more like a couple of guys the same age."

The degree to which he has screwed up his afterlife...

"You need my help, don't you?"

"Maybe. A little."

I await his next confession.

"Okay," he follows through. "Yes. If you could run some interference for me when grandma shows up, that would give me some breathing room to pull off the trick."

The first stop on my vacation in the sweet hereafter, and I am already forced to come up with excuses to conceal my identity.

"I can't make an appointment with her."

"Why not?"

I am tempted to reveal my secret just to see how much he is willing to accept, how far he is willing to go to preserve his own deception.

"It's just wrong," I say.

Which is true enough.

"Don't get all high and mighty on me," grouses the grandfather.

Retreat seems like the best option. I gulp the rest of my coffee and place the cup in the saucer as though ringing a closing bell.

"If you want to live your afterlife like a bedroom farce, that's your business," I rise to leave. "But keep me out of it."

"I should have known I couldn't rely on you," he hurls an insult from the sitting position.

I heave a slur of my own from the high ground.

"When I think of you, I always think of that silly song," I set him up. "But you're so much more than that. You're a silly man."

I imagine all the customers cheering my verbal kill shot, but none of them stop what they are doing. I think harder, demanding applause in my mind, but they continue to go about their business. I consider piling on with a crack about him talking like a working-class hero while refining his short game on his backyard putting green.

"What are you waiting for?" he asks before I can finish crafting the line.

"Nothing," I look around for something to excuse my hesitation.

I indeed find nothing and walk out of the shop.

"Just killing the moment," I mutter as I glare at my disobedient creations on my way out.

Walking the streets I wonder where all of these other creations come from, if the buildings and streets and cars are general responses to what I imagine when I think of the word "building" or "street" or "car", or if I have seen these specific versions before, if only for a second, and they were lying untapped in my subconscious waiting for a cue. Like I told the grandfather, I spent no time thinking about any of it, yet I created it. Maybe the administration provides stock backgrounds. We can only imagine so much, so they fill in our gaps.

I walk longer than necessary to distance myself from the delusions of magic fancied by a man whose DNA is intertwined with the DNA of the man whose genes I wear. I keep walking because I hope to reach the edge of whatever this is, to run into a wall, bump into a screen. I wonder how I would handle that revelation. Maybe bang on the wall and yell something melodramatic, or lean back against the screen and force a loud, cocky laugh upward, though I have no reason to assume those in charge are up above. They could be anywhere. Instead of bumping into the edge, I could fall off a ledge, never landing.

When I at last surrender the idea of my world being flat, I imagine somewhere to sit, as I feel tired, which makes me wonder why I would feel tired in a place of my own invention. Rather than sit, maybe I can make myself not feel tired anymore. But that would not be an accurate simulation. I felt jittery when I left the coffee house, but that may have been thanks to the conversation. I think of a bar. That way I can sit, and also find out if I can feel buzzed in this kingdom. A woman is about to walk past me and I stop her to ask if she has ever been to the bar I just made up. She says she has. I ask her for directions, and after she tells me how to get there, I ask her to describe it. Her description makes it sound like a dive bar for people who would rather not go to a dive bar, the same aesthetic as the coffee house I fabricated, only dressed up for a night out in Downtown Disney. I would say the kind of place where we scheduled meetings that took place after work hours, if work hours existed during crunch. All hours are work hours in crunch time, so I guess what it sounds like is the kind of place where we scheduled meetings in the dark.

She is correct. That is exactly what it looks like.

Chapter Four

In my empire of the mind, or soul, or spirit, or whatever its guiding essence may be, it is possible, it turns out, to get a buzz on. I try to push my high and achieve drunkenness, but there appear to be limits, which strikes me as a good idea. I wonder why there are limits on the effects of alcohol consumption and not on the effects of sexual conquests. Maybe there are, and Devin's grandfather has not reached his ceiling. If he has been exclusive with Angela, maybe the first one is a freebie. If he tries again with someone else, maybe he will not be able to perform. I wish I had not thought of that. To help me forget, I order another pilsner, because Devin prefers IPAs, before remembering I have reached my afterlife limit and I may as well have ordered a soda water. My awareness is lagging by a second or two thanks to the level at which I am holding steady.

The projections hanging out at the bar with me are impressive to a point. They are lifelike, and I have some decent conversations with a few of them, but I gather they cannot generate original ideas. Everything we talk about is borrowed from what I have of Devin in my head. They not only plagiarize the thoughts of those who created them, they agree with those thoughts. Or at least that is the case with me, as a clone of a man like Devin. I imagine there are residents who prefer to be disagreed with, who appreciate a good argument. But I suspect most are like Devin. Agreement and praise is their idea of heaven. I start to think maybe the recurring, vague familiarity of my conversations with my projections is the source of my time lag, rather than the alcohol brewed with an automatic kill switch built in.

If I could recover that second or two, I might be able to catch the woman at the end of the bar looking at me. Every time I look her way, she appears to be in the process of looking away. I try to make up for my boozy lag by looking at her a second or two faster, which makes sense to me, and that seems to work, but then realize I did not catch her looking. She is glaring at me, and her gaze is steady. I smile, but the result may not be warm or flirtatious, because when she walks my way, she looks like she is on her way to complain about something to someone, and I hope I am not that person. I face forward, focus on the bottles lining the back of the bar, and think small.

"This is going even worse than I imagined," she says from behind my back.

I turn my head far enough to see her out of one eye.

"I'm sorry," I say as a combination of question and statement, whichever works.

"I didn't expect you to be happy to see me, but I didn't expect you to pretend you don't know me."

"Jane," I remember the name from my slapdash orientation in the cubicle.

I face her, but keep my seat.

"Jane Lamar, yes?"

"Oh my God..." she shakes her head and looks down, around, anywhere but at me.

"I accepted your request," I defend myself, defend Devin.

She locks in on me, and behind her eyes appears to be shredding a list of things she wanted to say.

"Thank you, Devin," she strains to remain calm. "That's so sweet. I guess everyone I knew was wrong about you."

I check to see if she has a drink in her hand. She does not, so I brace myself for a slap. I take a good look at her and instead brace myself for a punch, to the face or to the gut, grateful I did not stand up.

She has so much she wants to say to Devin, so much she wants to do to me, she is overwhelmed, so she leaves.

I am relieved for a moment, then curious. Just how awful a person is my original?

I try to part the crowd with my mind, but again they refuse to obey.

Weaving through them, I reach the door and burst into the cool night air, catching sight of her walking away.

"Jane!" I call after her.

She maintains her pace.

"I'm sorry!" I apologize in stride and offer another apology when I reach her.

She stops and I gasp for air.

"I truly am," I squeeze in between breaths. "It's just, you know, dying young. I'm still adjusting. This is nice and all, but takes some getting used to. I don't know what to think, how to deal with any of it, anyone. My first appointment was a disaster."

"Who was it with?" she relents enough to ask.

"My grandpa," my heart rate is about back to normal.

She is not the least bit surprised. They were a serious enough couple to wade into the waters of each other's families. Her facial summary of his grandfather makes my heart race again, but with laughter rather than exhaustion.

As my joyful barking ebbs, and space opens up for conversation, I consider how deep Devin had to bury their relationship for her name not to register any reaction.

"You've obviously adjusted well," I tease her.

She avoids looking at me again, but this time as if pretending to look for a place to hide.

"Seriously, though," I say without trying to change the tone too much. "I'm sorry you had to move here so early."

"Well, you know, I wanted to get in before the real estate market took off."

"Good call."

"I've flipped a fair number of houses, invested in some commercial property."

"You always were savvy."

"Maybe too savvy."

I nod, able to read only so much into her references.

"I'd invite you back into my bar," I gesture to where we came from. "But do you want to go someplace more quiet?"

"Do you know anyplace?" she smiles.

"I can probably think of one," I play along.

"How about Gemini Brothers?"

I try to remain calm. This is starting to go so well.

"Sounds great," I exclaim with a bit too much enthusiasm.

I make a show of putting my fingers to my temples as if in deep concentration, which she appreciates.

"Just curious," I pry. "What is it you liked so much about that place?"

"I loved going there after seeing a movie," she reminisces. "I felt like it balanced out the evening."

"Me too," I grasp for something that may trigger a memory. "I loved the smell."

"Ooh, yes," she agrees. "I mostly read online now, but I still go with a book every so often just for the smell."

That does the trick. The name combined with the scent of books leads me to enough of a vision to piece something together. I have the storefront in mind, and a select few aisles.

"Shall we?" I sweep my arm forward with a slight bow, and she takes the first steps. I make sure the shop is around the first corner so our walk does not last long enough to become awkward.

"How did I do?" I ask as we enter.

"Close enough," she nods while surveying the interior.

We walk past the tables stacked with books labeled "Best Sellers", and I wonder where these books are selling so well. Heaven? Earth? Some other enclave of the universe? She gravitates toward the fiction shelves, and I follow.

"How did you get here so young?" I ask. "If you don't mind me asking."

"Cancer," she answers, as short and curt as if providing her middle initial.

"Oh..." I search for a deposit of her diagnosis in Devin's memory bank, in any amount, but find no record.

"You didn't hear about any of the fundraisers?" she probes.

"Well..." apparently he did not. "You know me."

"Just flyers in store windows and social media posts," she compiles probable causes of his ignorance, or what Devin might think of as excuses. "You know, places where people congregate."

"No press releases?"

"Maybe if I had been married to you," she slings without the slightest bit of nostalgia, a thought experiment and nothing more. "So what's your story? What punched your ticket?"

"I'm here by accident," I catch myself. "An accident. I was involved in an accident."

"What kind? Car? Plane?"

"I'm not sure, actually."

"You're not sure?"

"I guess it's one of those cases where the brain shuts down, saves you from experiencing something awful. I remember a pain in my neck. Maybe I choked on something."

"That tracks. I was a pain in your neck, and you didn't remember me."

She pauses and picks out a book to leaf through, but really wants to let her joke land. I acknowledge it with an air rim shot.

"Didn't they tell you at your orientation?" she asks.

"My orientation wasn't very helpful. Kind of disjointed. They were just as surprised as I was that I was here."

"Hmm," she puts the book back. "Maybe you did choke on something. Choking seems like it would be more unexpected than a lot of other accidents. Or maybe you were poisoned."

"I can imagine somebody wanting to do that to me."

"The organizers here would see it coming, though," she ignores my self-deprecation. "Don't you think? They would know there was a plot to poison you, and they'd be ready to greet you."

"I must have choked, then."

"That makes it sound like you missed a putt, or a free throw. Like you lost a game you should have won."

She rounds the corner into the next aisle.

"I kind of did," I follow her.

She looks over her shoulder at me.

"Something bad happen to your company?" she dangles something else I may be referring to.

"Not at all," I let her know.

She appreciates the implication, faces forward, and continues down the aisle.

I understand there is much more to learn about her. I have only known her for a half hour, and Devin knew her for who knows how long, probably years. But I am as disappointed in him as I am fascinated by her.

She stops and pivots in my direction, looking a lot less playful.

"Maybe this is too soon," she says.

"Okay," I hem. "Can I see you tomorrow?"

"No," she smiles. "That's not what I mean. I was thinking of running something by you, but then I thought maybe it should wait, and I'm thinking all of this out loud. You know, how I tend to do."

"I remember."

Of course I do not, but now that I know that about her, I will never forget.

"Since I've said that much out loud, I probably shouldn't keep you in suspense."

"Probably."

I am eager to pursue my education.

"Do you remember the procedure?" she asks.

I try to look as though the memory of whatever the procedure is will come to me in a moment, but she reads something else into my expression.

"I know, stupid question," she apologizes.

"No, no," I assure her. "No stupid questions around here. I told you how foggy I've been since I arrived, so it's perfectly reasonable for you to wonder how much I remember about life on the other side."

"Before the accident," she adds.

"Before I choked."

The reference does not resonate with her like it did before. I would offer my regrets for overusing it, but rather than sniffing to see if the metaphor has spoiled, she seems concerned with what she wants to tell me.

"Well," she wades into the procedure. "Sometimes I imagined what might have happened if any of them came to term, how they would have turned out if they had been born."

I furrow my brow and nod my head slowly to prevent my eyes from bulging and my head from shaking violently and to keep me from yelling "What!?"

They pursued some kind of in vitro fertilization together, and Devin left no recollection of it. I can see how her cancer could sneak past him, since it happened after their breakup, but trying to have a child is something they experienced together. My respect for him plummets even deeper. My shame over being some form of him skyrockets. I try to take pride in working to clean the slate.

"Did imagining how they might have turned out help?" I say to soothe her and myself, to avoid causing a scene. Not that any of the projections wandering around the bookstore would notice.

"Not really," she admits. "It just kept me thinking about the whole thing, and I needed to move on."

"Like I did."

I hope my self-loathing reaches its source. If Devin and I have any sort of shared mind, this is when he would feel it. Finding out what I am, and where I ended up, each within minutes of the other, between the launch and the afterlife orientation, may have been less intense compared to what I am learning in the book store.

"I wouldn't know," she sounds bitter for a moment. "Sorry. I don't want, no, that's not why I brought this up."

"I deserve any jab you want to throw at me."

"No," she insists. "Not again. That thing ruined our relationship, and now it's ruining this thing we have here, and it's always my idea."

She is so much better than the person I am supposed to be.

"What did you want to tell me about it?" I remind her.

She takes a deep breath.

"Like I said," she refocuses. "I couldn't help but wonder what might have been, so after I got here, I thought maybe I could create some projections."

"Oh..."

"Yup."

"Of the kids? The future kids?"

"Mm hmm."

"Did it work?"

She nods.

"Seriously?" I am flabbergasted. "I can't even make projections that applaud my one-liners or get out of my way. And the conversations..."

I fade into disgusted mumbling noises.

"It took me a while to get a feel for them in general," she explains. "And I asked management if it was okay to make these in particular, but yeah. I got their approval."

"What were they like? Or could have been like? If they existed? I don't even know how to word this question."

"Do you want to meet them?"

"You can conjure them up, just like that?"

"I can."

"And they are them? There are more than one?"

"I went all in. All seven embryos."

I am silent for at least seven seconds. I must have a look of wonder on my face, rather than the look of shock that feels just as likely, for the length of time does not appear to worry her.

"Sure," I cannot say no. "Let's go meet our kids."

"All at once?" she asks. "Or one at a time?"

"What would you recommend?"

"Either way has its advantages. All at once can be a little overwhelming. One at a time can get a little long, since it means running into each of them on occasion over the course of the night."

"I want to go all in. Like you did."

"All right," she leads the way. "Let's go out back."

"Out back," I follow. "There's an alley or something?"

"Something."

"You don't know?"

"You designed the place."

"I don't know what I did with the back."

"You'll think of something."

I keep pace as her stride accelerates.

She reaches the back door and thrusts the push bar with a conquering clack.

The back is indeed an alley, probably since that is what first came to mind when I asked.

Seven youngish adults are waiting for us. They look to be in their mid-twenties. Five are women and two are men.

"I went for an age that would give us a sense of how their lives were shaping up," she narrates as we approach.

Most of them look like they might live in the alley. A couple of them look more put together, but not by much.

We stop and face them. They may not be doing very well, but they seem friendly enough. I start to ask Jane how we proceed, but the young woman on the far left steps forward. She is one of the projections that appears to be slightly better off. She looks as though she might work at a diner that only serves breakfast and lunch in a neighborhood undergoing gentrification.

"Hi," she says, offering her hand.

"Hello," I reciprocate.

"I go by Jan."

"As opposed to Jane?"

I look over at Jane. She jerks her head toward the lineup, ordering me to pay attention.

"She let us choose our names," Jan says.

"Ah," I nod. "So...how are things in your life?"

"Not bad," she comes across as proud. "I was in a rough place for a while, but got clean thanks to some really awesome friends of mine."

"Glad to hear it."

"I started to feel stupid," she continues. "They had parents who ignored them, too. But their parents weren't around because they needed to work. Mine weren't around because they wanted to work."

"That sounds like quite a breakthrough."

I lean toward Jane.

"Do they know we're their parents?" I ask her through the corner of my mouth.

"In the abstract, yes," she does not try to keep her answer quiet. "But since they don't exist, it's nothing personal."

"That's a relief," I take her cue to not worry about being discrete.

"She's right," Jan says. "I don't blame you for anything. That's just who you were."

"Thank you?" I guess.

"Nice meeting you," Jan waves instead of shaking hands again so soon and shrinks back into the lineup.

"Do they ever call you Mom?" I ask Jane as the next one comes forward.

"Nope," she answers. "By design."

"Smart."

One of the two young men greets me and tells a similar story of neglect, of parents who were never there for him, only his version does not have a relatively happy ending. He is on the streets, relying on shelters and friends with couches for the occasional good night's sleep.

By about the fifth tale of parental indifference leading to a rootless life and an occasional, somewhat-inspiring redemption, I understand. These are not projections of what would have been their children. They are coping mechanisms. As the seventh sibling wraps up her story, the most dramatic of the bunch, saved for last for that reason, I wonder how much awareness Jane brings to her meetings with them.

"Well," I debate bringing it up with her as I bid farewell to the seven public service announcements shaped like human beings. "It was a pleasure meeting you all. I wish we could have done better by you. But that last story, I must say Amber, is impressive. I'm proud of you for not killing your pimp when you had the chance. Thank you, everyone, for sharing. Maybe we'll do this again sometime. Someplace nice."

We nod and grin at each other as they disperse in different directions.

When the alley is clear, I decide there is no good reason to question what Jane created, or even more important, why she created them.

"A lot to take in," she says.

I continue to stare in the direction one of them took on their way out, which is now empty.

"It is," I agree.

"Shall we call it a night?" she suggests.

I look at her. She may have met her projections before, but they still leave her with more than she can voice without first spending time in her thoughts. As much as I would like to go back inside and drift through the aisles with her, saying good night is the only option.

"Sure," I submit. "But I want to do this again. Not this exactly, with the kids, but you know, do something."

"Of course," she smiles. "Us young folks have to stick together here. It's like the biggest retirement community in the universe."

Deciding whether to kiss is no less touchy here than there. I make the move, but make it clear I am aiming for the cheek. She embraces the compromise.

"I want to see where this alley leads," I settle the matter of who goes back inside the bookstore.

She offers one more smile before disappearing through the door.

I walk the alley, but see none of it. I entertain the possibility of every single one of their children turning out the way she made them, the odds that her method of moving past her relationship with Devin really does represent an accurate prediction of an alternate future. When I find myself back on a busy street, I look around to see if any of her manifestations are there, maybe holding up a sign that says they are hungry, or playing a guitar out of tune with a paper cup of change laid out in front of them as bait.

I need a place to stay for the night. Thinking of Devin's house summons a meager selection of imagery, so I come up with a place of my own. I base it on the home of an investor we visited, a basic two-story, three-bedroom that emphasized the yard more than the house. She had lived there since before the neighborhood became renowned. The half-acre lot is not the kind of place that fits in a downtown setting, so I have to walk for a while to reach it.

I stand in the dark living room staring out at the lighted patio, strings of bulbs casting a soft glow over a well-groomed seating area that gives way to a garden in the shadows teeming with shrubs and trees that appear to have grown wild, until a closer look reveals the patterns. I sip a beer and think about how this house was built in a moment, how there was never any land with nothing on it, then a cement foundation laid, then a wood frame raised, then walls, and a roof, until at last the house was complete, then furnished, to the point where I now stand, in this space, staring at all that has been constructed. Instead it just appeared. I stomp my feet on the floor, tap on the glass door. It feels solid. I wonder what it is made of.

As I walk up to the second floor to find a bedroom, I notice the stairs are silent, no creaks or pops, and consider whether this is an oversight by the producers or by me. As soon as I think of it, the stairs start popping.

When I lie down, I have the sensation of floating, despite feeling the bed underneath me. I float away from what Jane has done to try to move on, her afterlife family of worst case scenarios, and explore the idea that Devin may have been so hurt by their failed attempt to have children that he worked hard to bury the memory, to make it go away, harder than he ever worked on anything made to stay.

Chapter Five

After spending a lot of time lying in the dark, I close my eyes. When I open them, daylight floods the room. I may have dozed for a minute, I may have slept for hours. Sleep may not be necessary here. I went through the ritual out of habit. I gather the point is to reset the program rather than rest. With a day behind me, however a day may be defined, I feel emboldened to try someplace I have never been before, which is everyplace in the world outside of the valley surrounding our company headquarters.

I imagine what I think Hawaii must look like. People really like going there. Devin has some memories of it, though for the most part they are confined to the inside of a conference room. Pens and pads of paper feature the name of the hotel, but none of the images in mind focus on them. They are always in the background, and the font is curly and difficult to read. The name appears to start with the letter P. It could be The Plumeria, as in the flower, or the word "Premier", which might be the name of the ownership group rather than the resort itself. I can make out the name "Maui" on several items, so I run with that particular island, figuring the more specific, the better. I step outside hoping to already be there, but I am in front of the house in the neighborhood I walked through last night.

A compact sedan pulls up and the driver asks if I called for a ride to the airport. I am about to tell him I have no phone, but then feel a vibration in my pocket. I reach for the source, which is a phone with a message about my ride being here. I wave it at him and get in the backseat. We barely have a chance to exchange greetings before we arrive at the airport, which is a small, regional type that can only host airplanes of a certain size. I am suspicious.

"How long is the flight to Maui?" I ask.

"Not long."

"How long is not long?"

"As long as it needs to be."

Another fruitless conversation with a projection. I get out and the driver tells me to not forget my suitcase. The trunk pops open and there is indeed a small suitcase inside. I take it and walk into the terminal. The flight is boarding. Through the window I see a jet that is larger than the building. I get in line, and it moves quickly. I am on the plane with my bag stored in the overhead bin within minutes.

After takeoff, we are served mimosas and omelets. After the service cart clears our trays and glasses, we are handed hot towels. Then we land.

When I step outside the airport in what is supposed to be Maui, a shuttle bus embossed with the name of the hotel is waiting at the curb. They went with "The Plumeria Premier Resort", which is a stupid name, but I have only myself to blame. If I had been more decisive, the producers would not have to split the difference. We drive along some picturesque coastline on our way to the hotel. There is no line to check in, and by the time I am in my room staring out at the ocean, I estimate no more than an hour has passed since I walked out the front door of the investor's house. I wonder if I should make that house my home after my trip to this island is over. I wonder what is in my suitcase.

I open it and find a travel kit spread across the top layer, which leads to a moment of pondering whether tooth brushing is any more necessary than sleep, or if it is another ritual preserved to help ground the production. I toss it aside to check out the clothes underneath. They are a collection of clichés. I choose the pair of white pants, rather than the white shorts, and the Hawaiian shirt that happens to be on top of the others. I grab the espadrilles from the inside pocket, rather than the flip flops, and make a mental note to see if feet can be made more attractive in this realm than they were before.

The hotel lounge has a bar facing an open window looking out at the Pacific. Few people are taking advantage of it. I have a seat and am on the verge of ordering a beer when the bartender informs me hotel guests are entitled to a free daiquiri. I take them up on it. The sparse attendance makes it easy to listen to the surf. I never hear a blender before my drink is delivered. Either they are premade and kept frozen, or simply appear, as things tend to do here.

"Devin Orr," a flat male baritone says to my right.

I turn to find man about my age standing by extending his hand.

"Hello," I shake his hand, which feels older than mine.

"Phil Dedmon," he introduces himself.

"Ah, Phil," I recall.

"Mind if I sit down?" he asks.

"Please," I gesture toward the seat next to me. "The office jockeys at my orientation really got a kick out of your name."

"It comes in handy around these parts," he says. "Makes for a good ice breaker."

"Projections get the joke?"

"Most of them," he shrugs, a motion that suits him well. "Thanks for taking my request. People are hard to come by at our age."

"Of course. Come here often?"

"I know my way around," he tries on a different shrug. "One advantage of having an empty dance card is you end up with plenty of time to get to know the place."

"Yeah," his sense of place reminds me. "What's with the little journeys from one place to another? Cars, airplanes, shuttle buses. They could clearly just let us be somewhere without the fanfare."

"Provides a sense of place," his shoulders continue to get a workout. "A sense of putting in some effort. Like in game design, right? You make a map of the territories, you want players to get to know it, not just be in that place, snap! Or that other place, pow! They need to get there, even if it's a short ride."

"Were you on one of our design teams?"

"I was in Maintenance and Operations."

"We contract that out once a game is up and running."

"No, Maintenance and Operations as in keeping the buildings on your corporate campus clean and climate-controlled."

"Oh, sorry. That sounded so out of touch."

"It's cool."

"So self-absorbed," I admonish Devin from beyond.

"No, really. It's okay."

"And we met?"

"Two times," he nods. "Once when I was testing the smoke detector in your office, the other time when I changed all the bulbs on the string of lights hanging over the balcony outside your office."

"They were all burnt out?"

"No," he seems reluctant to say anymore.

"What?" I pry.

"Well," he straightens up for the big reveal. "You changed one yourself, which was nice. You were trying to keep from having to call us. But the glow of the replacement bulb didn't match the rest, and it drove you nuts, so I changed them all for you since doing that would take more time than you had to spare."

"Oh dear God," I put my head in my hands.

"It wasn't that bad," he slumps back into his standard stoop. "It was easier than putting up a new string of lights."

"Devin should remember you."

"You're Devin."

"Right," I come up for air. "Us rich, egotistical people like to refer to ourselves in the third person sometimes. I guess from seeing our name in print so often? I don't know."

"Lesser people than you have forgotten me."

"Please tell me when you died, we did something nice for you and your family."

"I wasn't with the company when I died. I had taken a job with the city by then."

"I don't blame you."

"It had nothing to do with the way I was treated. Working for you was fine. I just liked the variety of the city job. I could go to different buildings and neighborhoods, instead of being in the same place all the time."

"Sounds like a good move."

"Good enough," he pulls another from his collection of shrugs.

We pause to take a sip from our drinks and look and listen to the ocean.

"What other obnoxious things did you catch me doing or saying?" I ask.

"Nothing much," he sneaks in another sip.

"Come on, you can tell me."

"I'm not one to talk out of turn."

"You're not. I asked for it."

He stares above the ocean, at the top of the window frame. I assume he is considering whether to tell me more, though he may be deciding which of the many embarrassing stories to share.

"This one time," he chooses, "you said something I thought was pretty funny, but the person you said it to thought it was obnoxious, I guess. He was about to tell you something, and he said that thing people like to say beforehand, you know how they say 'Correct me if I'm wrong', and you said 'Oh I most certainly will' before he even said what he had to say. I overheard it while I was cleaning out someone's desk and kind of laughed to myself, but the guy you said it to walked away and passed by all mumbling and grumbling."

"No guesswork there, Phil. He definitely thought it was obnoxious."

"And this other time..." he remembers another story. "Actually it wasn't one time, it was something you would do a lot."

"Oh, really?"

"Yeah," he breezes past any of his initial discomfort. "You spent a lot of time in the company gym, but you'd do exercises you could do at home."

"Like what?"

"Like stomach crunches and pushups. Stuff like that. You'd get all dressed up in your workout clothes, find a space in the middle of the equipment, then huff and puff away."

"And people would roll their eyes when they knew I wasn't looking."

"Pretty much."

"I could spin that to say I gained inspiration from other people."

"You could."

"I was always good at generating my own PR. That much I know. I was made for it."

I bask in my first moment of purpose since discovering what I am. Pitching Devin and his company to the press and to investors was the meaning of my existence.

"I want to find more good in my past," I think out loud. "But I'm not sure that's possible."

I am surprised for a moment that I managed to say "my" past instead of "his" past, and relieved I avoided creating confusion so soon, but then I had no past of my own until I passed into this place.

Even if I did slip, Phil may not notice. He looks as though he could stare at the ocean until last call, if this lounge has a last call.

"Forgive me," I try to get his attention. "My whining is ruining the view."

"Don't worry about me," he swats away my apology. "That's what I always say. And I mean always. It's my motto. It was my pitch back on earth, too, since we're talking about the past. Forget I'm here, or cry on my shoulder. It's all good. I'm never uncomfortable. I didn't always say it, but it was always clear to anyone I was with."

"Did you make a lot of friends that way?"

"No," he says. "Not really."

"Well, I sure appreciate it."

"Thanks," he raises his glass in my direction. "I guess most people want at least a little drama. Some more than others. Oh well."

"Oh well," I raise my glass in his direction.

We drink.

"Hey," I think of something mid-sip. "Since we may have a long wait until the rest of our generation gets here, is it possible to look up relatives from way back when? Like a great-great-great grandparent? I was overwhelmed at my orientation, so I never thought to ask."

"I asked," Phil turns his gaze back out to the sea.

I wait for him to tell me their answer.

"And?" I prompt.

"Hmm? Oh...yeah. I wasn't that concerned with having a lot of people to hang out with. I was just interested."

"What did they say?"

"No go."

"Really?"

"Yup."

"Why? What was the reason?"

"They said it was for the best."

"That's it? That's all they said?"

"That's what I said," he says. "I said 'that's it?' And then they said something else."

"What did they say?"

"They said it was a different time."

"It was a different time..." I repeat the sentence with relish.

"I got it, the more I thought about it."

"Yes," I consider why I might be enjoying that answer. "I think I get it too. I wonder how far back that rule goes."

"I have a great-grandfather I hang out with."

"Oh yeah?"

"We have a ranch we made together in Northern Idaho."

"Nice."

"It is. He's a nice guy. I met him when I was a kid. Maybe that's the rule. Nobody you haven't met in person."

"Does he appear as the age you remember him?"

"He does. Every time we say good bye he jokes about going off to be young again."

"Which is probably true."

"Definitely true."

I almost ask him if his great-grandfather cheats on his great-grandmother and asks you to cover for him, but we have only conversed for a matter of minutes, and as successful a talk as this may be, that may be taking our talk too far, too fast. The impulse to discuss dirty old men abides, though, and leads me in a different direction.

"I wonder what cavemen used to do when they got here," I ride my daiquiri deeper into the mysteries of the afterlife timeline.

"Make sure the hunting was good, the weather was perfect."

"The berries were always ripe. No seasons."

"Fire was easy to make. Maybe they allowed them some matches."

"How far back do you think this organization goes?"

"Like when they started bringing people over?" Phil asks.

"Yeah. Did they bring them over before they were people? Did they start with little mammals that survived the meteor?"

"Maybe. I mean, that would be an easy place to start. Give them a chance to grow the company, sharpen up the simulations."

"I can't imagine the office has always looked like it does."

"No way," Phil agrees. "How do you explain that to the cave people?"

"Your whole orientation would be taken up trying to explain what the chairs and tables are made out of, or how a stapler works."

"I wonder if any of them are still around."

"The cave people?" I confirm.

"Yeah."

"I could see that happening. They probably don't get bored as easily as we do. If the hunting and fishing are good, and the nuts and berries are there for the gathering, they might be happy doing what they do forever."

"Or it might be too easy," Phil suggests. Not to disagree, just to put it out there with a shrug.

"The struggle to survive can be quite a rush, I imagine. It certainly offers purpose."

"If it's not the cave zone, I wonder what the longest-running simulation is."

"I'll bet it is the cave zone."

"I wouldn't take that bet. I think you're right. There's gotta be at least one cave person left."

"If not the cave zone, I'm thinking it's an age with a massive amount of misery, where the people are really glad to get out of there and into some paradise."

"Like some time that had a plague," Phil spitballs. "Or a bunch of slavery."

"Or both. Yeah. Horrible times. Like, you know, most of human history."

"So who knows?"

"Who knows?"

We raise our drinks and toast to not knowing, like we did when we said "Oh well".

I have a feeling Devin never had a conversation like this with anyone before, because as the night grows older, and we happen upon one haphazard topic after another, none of the warmth or laughter or teasing trips any memories. After every pointless observation that means everything in the moment, I lean back in some way, in my chair or in my head, and brace myself for a recollection to drop. Around the time the moon is over the ocean, I stop searching for signs of Devin and bask in knowing this friendship is all mine, and he never had one like it.

We never leave the hotel lounge. When we agree to quit for the night, Phil apologizes for keeping me from Maui.

"Doesn't matter," I assure him. "It's not even Maui. It's just a four-dimensional version of my shirt."

I look down at it and trace the palm trees.

"Check it out tomorrow," Phil encourages me. "I'll leave you alone. I promised my great-grandpa I'd hang out at the ranch with him."

"I guess it's not every day you can see how your island turned out," I look on the bright side.

"Come up to the ranch sometime," he says.

"Up..." I ponder.

"I'm used to thinking of Idaho as being north."

"Still?"

"I'm earthy."

"Grounded," I play along.

"Seriously, though. Come visit."

"Indeed I will. It sounds wonderful."

Phil opens his arms for a hug as though I hit a game-winning home run and he is waiting for me at home plate. I join in the celebration of my accomplishment, though I am sure to him it is just another good night.

Chapter Six

Maui seems to have turned out well. I rent a motor scooter and at one of the stops on my way around the perimeter, I hear one projection of a tourist say to another that the island is just like they remember it, which is nice of them, but also their job.

I would like to see Jane. Now that I am gaining a sense of what friendship is like, I feel as though I can develop a healthy relationship with her. Maui would be too suggestive. We need to be someplace casual, where people happen to meet, rather than a destination. The house I made is in a neighborhood that must have a park nearby. I fly back to make sure it does. The flight seems even shorter this time, and not because of a tail wind.

The park is easy to make compared to a Hawaiian island. I sit on a bench along the main path and focus my attention on the people to see how well they turned out. For the sake of studying them and gathering ideas on how to make improvements, I try not to think of them as projections. I recall one of the game designers at Devin's company talk about how much she liked to people watch. She is really going to like it here when her time comes.

One of the first patterns I note is that their collective movement is too smooth, as if designed by a civil engineer used to thinking of ways to keep traffic flowing through a variety of intersections. I discover one person who moves against the grain, because he really is a person.

Devin's grandfather approaches in a black blazer and black V-neck t-shirt, but stops ten yards before reaching me. He keeps his eyes fixed on mine, and without a word, pulls a scarf from the breast pocket of his jacket, and a golf ball from the side pocket. He holds the ball up in front of him, covers it with the scarf, then snaps the scarf away to reveal his hand is empty. He wiggles his fingers and twirls his hand to emphasize that the ball gone. Having established the disappearance of the golf ball, he flaps his hand and the ball reappears between his thumb and index finger. He brings the ball up to his eye like a monocle, tosses it up in the air, and it appears to vanish before coming down. And with that, he raises his arms as if acknowledging applause, which there is none, then turns to leave, still never having said a word.

My first thought is that some of the people should have noticed him, but then reconsider. Pretending not to notice the crazy man performing street magic may be more accurate. For an even more lifelike simulation, they would need to notice him but make obvious efforts to look at anyone, anything else.

As I deliberate the best way to epitomize people who want to be left alone trying to ignore people who want to be noticed, another real person appears who may be drawing plenty of attention from those around her, but I would not know, because I am too focused on her.

Jane waves and smiles on her way toward me, and while she does not stop ten yards in front of me to make a golf ball disappear, that is about the point where her expression turns quizzical.

"I think I saw your grandfather pass by," she aims her thumb over her shoulder.

"You did see my grandfather pass by. Did he see you?"

"No," she sits down next to me. "He wasn't noticing anything. He seemed very happy about something."

I hesitate telling her the truth for a moment, then remind myself I am already a living, breathing lie, and have to decide whether to adopt a "what's one more?" mindset or "never again", or at least "as few as possible". I run with truth, as much as I may be kidding myself it matters.

"His magic act is really coming together."

"His magic act?"

I nod.

"Did he show you?"

"That's all he did."

"And then he scampered off?"

I nod again, re-creating the silence of his appearance.

She finds that funny.

"I'm one to talk," she amends her indulgence. "One of the first things I did when I got here was develop an act."

I am stunned and delighted.

"You did?"

"A performing dog show."

"My God…"

"Can you believe it?"

"I want to so badly. Show me. Please."

"It's in Las Vegas."

"You're still doing it?"

"I sold it to another dog trainer. My mentor, actually. I caught his show when he was still alive. I trained with him to perfect the act for five months, performed it for two months, then gave it up."

"What for?"

She seems to brush past her customary answer in search of a more entertaining one.

"The dogs," she decides. "I enjoyed the act, but started to think my goodness, I'm stuck with these dogs forever. An actual eternity."

"They were just projections of dogs, right?"

"Still, you know how it is. Dogs are far more sympathetic than people. I couldn't just let them disappear. I thought of having a final performance where the dogs would be raffled off to the audience members, but that would just be a more elaborate way of letting them disappear. So I spoke with Gustav, who it turns out had been thinking of changing up his act anyway, or so he told me, and we made the arrangements. Shall we go see it?"

"It won't be the same without you up there."

"The dogs are the stars. That's one of the reasons I chose the act. I wanted the feeling of performing, of being on stage, but didn't feel like I had any talent. All I needed was patience to train the dogs, then

I could hide behind them when the show was up and running. Road trip?"

"How long is the drive to Vegas in this joint?"

"If I drive, maybe fifteen minutes."

"You drive fast."

"I know a shortcut."

Within minutes of exiting the green leafy streets of my neighborhood, we are driving through the desert. Minutes after that, the Las Vegas skyline looms in the distance. More surprising is the lack of traffic. Devin has an aggravating memory of being stuck in traffic on Las Vegas Boulevard that is placated by the wide open streets populated by enough cars and people to make the city feel inhabited, but not cramped.

We pull into a parking structure behind one of the massive casinos and walk through its adjacent shopping mall to a quaint little theater in the midst of several luxury restaurants. A line about a dozen deep has formed waiting for the theater doors to open.

"Cute," I remark.

"You didn't think I played the main stage at the MGM Grand?"

"I didn't think of the venue at all. Now that we're here, this makes perfect sense."

"Everything here is perfect," she says with enough seasoning to bring out the sarcasm.

The breach surprises me.

"Dinner after the show?" she veers back into sincerity and gestures at the surrounding options.

"Absolutely," I accept, and we stand together in line.

The doors open and the matron of the house emerges to scan tickets. I turn to ask Jane if she has already made arrangements, but she is looking ahead at the lady, anticipating eye contact. The ticket taker keeps her head down, focusing on the connection between the screen in her hand and the customers, and the beep which consummates the relationship.

When we reach the front of the line with nothing to scan, she looks up with suppressed irritation that turns to unabashed joy upon seeing Jane. They hug and squeal, agree that it has been too long since they have seen each other, and try to outdo one another over who is more happy about being reunited.

Jane gets around to introducing me when it comes time to keep the line moving. I receive an enthusiastic handshake while she reminds Jane where to find the reserved seats.

We are in the front row, off to one side, as though in position to take the stage if needed. The house fills up in about half the time it took us to drive here. As the lights dim, I expect an announcement about the very special guest in the audience, but the voice over the speakers sticks with the usual spiel about keeping electronic devices off, and that the show runs straight through without an intermission. I gather dogs are hard to refocus after they have a break.

There is a bigger variety of dogs than I expected. I assumed most of them would be small, so they are easier to put on platforms and ladders and bicycle seats, but there is an impressive mix, and the trainer hardly ever lifts them. They run and take their places on their own. They also bark with enthusiasm more than I would have thought. Concentration seems to come more naturally to dogs than to people. Whatever they do, that is what is on their mind, so a little barking here and there makes no difference.

About twenty minutes into the show, Jane leans over and says she needs to use the restroom. I am certain that is not why she is excusing herself.

Even though I see it coming, when it actually does happen, the moment is still electric.

Gustav announces to the dogs, rather than to the audience, that an old friend is back for a visit. When Jane enters from backstage, the dogs are overcome with joy. Their recognition of her convinces me that dogs make better projections than people. The audience tries to keep up with the dogs by applauding with gusto when Gustav finally introduces her to the people.

Jane harnesses the heightened energy of the dogs into a show that surpasses what her mentor and heir provided earlier. She even bows better than him at the conclusion of the show, as the dogs bounce and bark around her, and the audience demands a curtain call.

When we sit in a lounge alongside the promenade of the casino shopping mall afterwards, sipping blended, bright-colored drinks through straws, she suspects aloud that the talent discrepancy between her and Gustav is part of the afterlife package.

"I didn't specify that I should look better by comparison," she says. "But that kind of thing is probably baked in."

I am fascinated by the dogs, their design, and how much they remind me of real dogs.

"Do you think animals have anything like this?" I gesture around us, referring to the afterlife in general, not the casino retail center in particular.

"Doggie heaven?" she confirms. "Kitty heaven?"

"Hamster heaven?"

"That's the first problem," she says. "Where it ends. Goldfish? Ant farms? Petri dishes?"

"There's more than one problem?" I am intrigued.

"The bigger one is overpopulation. Animals focus on the tennis ball, on the patch of sunlight. They don't wonder if they should be doing more with their life. When would they ever choose stardust?"

"They could help prove whether space is infinite."

She smiles at my suggestion, but appears preoccupied.

"I want to level with you," she does not keep me guessing. "I didn't start this show because of a deep love for dogs or animals. They're nice.

I like them. But they weren't the point. Neither was a lifelong desire to perform."

I wait and let her continue.

"I saw this show with my family before I died," she says. "The kids loved it."

"Your kids?"

"My kids."

"How many did you have?" I catch myself. "Do you have?"

"That's okay," she assures me. "Might as well use the past tense. Might as well say 'did.'"

She takes a sip of her once-gaudy drink, its slushy texture turned to water.

"I did have two girls."

I hold off on searching for something to say and let the words come to me.

"Do you ever spend time with projections of them?" I ask.

"Nope," the colored water does not go down easily. "Nor my husband. The show is as close as I dare to get. I don't want fake versions of them. It's going to be weird enough when I finally see them for real, much later, decades from now. I won't recognize them. Especially the kids. We won't know each other. Maybe they offer to spend time with me as little girls, but that wouldn't be the real them. They'd be adults in kids' bodies. Why would I do that to them?"

She shudders.

"That's messy," she tries to end on a light note, but it feels wrong.

"You'll get to know them as adults," I refuse to play along.

"They'll catch me up on all the years I missed. All...what, seventy of them? Eighty?"

"You wouldn't have lived that long," I try to help. "Even if you lived to a ripe old age, you're still missing out on maybe thirty or forty years of their lives. And you'd still be meeting them after they've been old people. Like pretty much everyone else here."

"You're sweet," she stirs the lurid brew in her goblet. "Calling the whole system into question, tearing it down for my sake."

"Afterworld problems."

She almost laughs, but is once more thwarted by her second thoughts.

"You see why I can't be more than friends with you," she says, a statement worded as a question.

"I don't want to compromise your situation any more than you do," I promise. "Well, maybe a little more."

She smiles and looks away, her smile widening in conjunction with the rate at which she turns from me. The pose stirs a memory, the first one from Devin starring her. I reach for more, or at least some context for this particular image. Is this what she looked like when he first fell for her? Or when she broke up with him? Maybe it was a random moment that burrowed into his memories because of how open and mysterious she looks at the same time, or because she looks simply stunning.

"What?" she inquires after my gaze.

"Nothing," I fall back into where we are. "I was counting the hundreds of other excellent reasons to not be more than friends with me."

I am being honest, but it reads well enough as a joke, which I let carry the moment.

We leave the leftovers of our drinks to be poured down the drain, if that is necessary in an imaginary casino. The fifteen-minute drive home feels longer than the actual drive between Las Vegas and Silicon Valley. The hush between us makes the condensed desert seem as vast as the real Mojave, as forlorn as the good-nights we wish each other after I crawl out of the passenger seat.

I stare at myself in the mirror before going to bed. It is the first time I have looked at myself since I arrived. I have not worried about how I look. Even now, my reflection is a means to meditate rather than a search for stray hairs and blackheads. I glance at the toilet. I have yet to use one of those, either. I wonder if anyone uses them here. I know someone who will have the answer to that question.

I reach for the phone in my pocket and realize I never got Phil's number. I open the text app and write his name in the contact box and send a message.

He gets it.

Chapter Seven

The ranch Phil conceived with his great-grandfather overlooks a large lake, the spectacular result of massive glaciers jockeying for position in a valley of their own creation millions of years ago, and the memory of a ninety year-old man. I look at it through the kitchen window as Phil and I stand drinking coffee. I consider asking him the name of the lake, but it is unlikely to be an exact replica of whatever lake inspired it, so I take another sip instead. I relish the liquid heat and let it fuel my question.

"Does anyone ever take a dump here?"

Phil is never fazed.

"We put in a bathroom downstairs."

"I mean here in the afterworld, the whole place."

"If someone wants to."

"Why would they want to?"

"I heard a guy at your company say he did his best thinking on the toilet."

"Do you remember who it was?"

"I didn't know many names."

"So bowel movements aren't necessary, but if they inspire comfort or creativity, then by all means."

I raise my mug in tribute.

Phil clicks his mug to mine.

"Sometimes coffee isn't enough," he supplements my toast.

We revel in our warm gulps and take in the view.

"As I was texting you to see if it worked," I say. "I thought about our last conversation."

"Why's that?"

"Using the afterworld wonder phone made me remember something you said about cavemen and matches. And that got me to thinking maybe the reason leadership wants to keep generations apart at a certain point isn't because of perspective, of racism or sexism, but technology."

"Hmm," Phil either contemplates what I might mean, or humors me.

"One generation having technology the other doesn't have would be a logistical nightmare. Management doesn't want to worry about mixing Ancient Egypt with air conditioning, or, I don't know, the Roman Empire and AR-15s."

"And the cave people. Think of the cave people."

"It always comes back to the cave people."

"If they allowed people to visit to the cave place," Phil speculates, "you'd not only have to leave behind any technology, but also not bathe or shave for months to get ready."

"Which, to be fair, would only take about one day here. What if you need glasses to see?"

"Wish for better eyesight."

"But if you're more comfortable in your glasses…" I posit.

"Why would someone prefer to wear glasses?"

"For the same reasons someone insists on taking unnecessary dumps."

"Then wish for better eyesight just for the trip."

"What about a caveman who can't see very well," I switch perspectives. "Do the administrators let them in on that technology?"

"Glasses?"

"I know it's hard to think of glasses as technology these days."

"They probably just give them better eyesight on arrival."

"Then why not other perks? Running shoes? Refrigeration? Mouthwash?"

"I think they let them work with what they know. They build the best world with the tools they have."

"But with perfect eyesight and health."

"Maybe they learn things here. In their version of here. They come up with inventions we never did."

"Whole new timelines," I consider the possibility. "New directions leading to versions of the world we wouldn't recognize. Maybe this world is as real as ours."

"I used to hear people at your company talk about the multiverse," Phil recalls. "Is that what we've stumbled upon?"

"None of them ever talked about that with me."

"They didn't see you as a fellow geek."

My Devin Brain gets defensive.

"Being a geek and being smart aren't necessarily the same thing."

"I meant it as a compliment."

I swing our conversation back around to its opening.

"You really don't buy technology as the reason for the afterlife being a generational confederacy," I give him one more chance to agree with me. "You're convinced it's culture."

Rather than answer, he turns his head toward the kitchen door.

"Double G!" He calls.

"Great Grandpa?" I ask.

He nods.

"Philip!" the old man appears in the kitchen doorway, a throwback to the days when men kept office supplies in the breast pocket of their shirt. "You're here!"

We rotate to face him.

"I invited my friend Devin up to see the ranch."

"Hello," I put down my mug and extend my hand. "Devin Orr."

"Orr..." he shakes my hand mulls over my name. "That's a Scottish name. Northern English."

"Yes. Some cold place in that part of the world, I believe."

He releases his grip and sizes me up.

"You don't look like it."

"I haven't traced my family tree very far back."

"Got some mixed blood in you?"

"I guess so. A proud American mutt."

"I've got an app on my phone…"

He reaches into his shirt pocket but Phil interrupts.

"I was about to show Devin the dock," Phil pats me on the back and gestures to follow him out of the kitchen.

"Nice to meet you, Double G," I bid as I pass him by.

He does not respond. He is on his phone, presumably typing my last name into his genealogy app.

Phil waits until we are on the path to the lake to plead his case.

"I barely remember meeting him before he died," he says to me over his shoulder as he leads the way through a corridor of pine trees. "I was four years old. I didn't know him that well, but I was fascinated with how far back his life went. I don't think many people here have a bigger generation gap than we do. So he's got a bit of that thing management kept using to deny my request to meet anyone even older."

"It was a different time," I repeat the line.

"Still," Phil changes his tone. "We get along fine."

"Fine? You made it sound like such a warm relationship when you mentioned it in Maui. He seems more like your closing argument for why the producers build a border wall between the age brackets."

We emerge into a clearing just shy of the lake.

"I'll admit," Phil breathes in the lake air. "I come here mainly for the entertainment."

"What do you do, read him the current stats on interracial marriage?"

Phil chuckles.

"That does sound like fun."

We reach the dock and walk over the water.

"So what is the fun part?" I ask. "The entertainment."

"The reason he wanted to build this ranch," he raises his arms as if trying to part the waters of the lake. "That's the fun part."

"He didn't build it to hang around with you?"

He lowers his arms with a snort and sits on the edge of the dock.

"He lets me use it because I helped him. Since I worked in Maintenance and Operations, he figured I could lend some expertise. The real reason he built it was to be near the resort."

"The resort..." I join him on the edge, our feet dangling inches above the surface.

"He worked there for three seasons when he was a young man trying to figure out his life. To quote him, he 'got more tail than you can shake a stick at' during those summers. Every summer after that must have been a disappointment, because he spends all of his days here as a young man again, working that resort."

"What does he do there?"

"Bartends, bellhops, cleans the pool..."

"Gets tail."

"More than you can shake a stick at."

"I've never tried shaking a stick at tail. Maybe if we tried, one of us could beat him at his own game. Shake a stick at way more tail than he got."

"I guess he also has a room at the resort, because I've never met any of the women, and never seen him as a young man."

"Where does your great-grandmother fit into this?"

"I've never met her, either. She died before I was born. But I asked him about that, and he said they have an agreement."

"An agreement?"

"He does his thing, she does hers. Again, that's a quote."

"The quote would be 'I do my thing, she does hers.'"

"I grilled him on the agreement once, asked him what Great Grandma does on her end, and he got real touchy. 'What are we supposed to do up here?' he yelled, 'Float around on a cloud? Eat grapes? What the hell kinda paradise is that?' He might have said something about playing a harp or sitting on a throne. I just remember him screaming about heaven stereotypes. I don't think it was a happy marriage."

"Maybe they met at the resort," I propose. "And they role play, reenact the time they met, over and over."

"That's looking at the bright side. Or the dark side."

I look across the lake and let the sunlight flickering off the water fill my eyes, which makes the pine trees teemed on the mountains look as though they are strung with lights for Christmas.

"The afterlife," I murmur, "is a dirty old man's paradise."

"I don't think it's just old men," Phil sounds as though he is falling into a minor meditative trance along with me. "I think it's pretty perverted in general."

"Have you done anything to contribute to that opinion?" I talk to the lake and the trees as much as I talk to Phil.

"No," he says with neither self-righteousness nor embarrassment. "I have this funny feeling someone is watching, that this isn't really the afterlife. It's a test."

"The earth wasn't the test?"

"You can't do whatever you want on earth."

"You may be on to something, my friend."

The splashes of light in my eyes blend into a wave that overwhelms the water and the trees.

"You may be on to something," I repeat.

"Hello!" I hear a familiar voice coming from behind us on the land's end of the dock.

I cannot place its tone or timbre, but the poor timing and intrusion feed my recollection.

"Shooter!" the voice bellows.

That explains it.

The light falls from my eyes and I turn to see Devin's grandfather strutting toward us.

"I was having trouble finding the place," he explains in stride. "But then I got a signal. You were talking about me. I'm flattered."

"We were talking about your category," I remain seated. "The kind of men you're lumped together with."

"Uh oh," he pretends to be alarmed as he reaches us.

"Phil," I look over at him with a languid expression to let him know he need not get up. "This is my grandfather."

"Hello," Phil holds his ground.

"No deck of cards?" I ask the grandfather before he can bother Phil.

"No time to waste," he says. "We're on."

"What do you mean?"

"What do I mean? C'mon. Grandma's in town. She died yesterday. Didn't you make an appointment?"

I hang my head and sigh with enough exasperation to ripple the water under my feet. I want to confess, tell him I never got the message because I never met the woman, and to meet her now would kill her, if killing was possible in this world, since the person I am supposed to be is still alive.

"I won't make an appointment with her until you come clean with her," I say instead.

"I knew it."

"Then why did you come here?"

"I thought maybe I could find a shred of decency in that cold heart of yours."

His accusation is too melodramatic to land with any authority. I pause and assess what a real indictment might sound like.

"Were you like this when you were alive?" I ask.

"If you had visited more often, you would know."

I focus on the lake again. If I look at him, I may spew the whole situation, and ruin my chance at whatever management is debating as my fate.

"Maybe you and grandma can come to an agreement," I suggest.

Phil horselaughs.

"What do you mean by that?" the grandpa bristles.

"Maybe she wouldn't mind letting you prance around with your side piece if she could do the same."

"Are you kidding?"

"Maybe she won't be as heartbroken as you think she'll be. Maybe your affair will provide her with an excuse to do her own thing, create her own paradise that has nothing to do with you."

"You sound like her sister," he snarls. "I'll bet that bitch already met with her and trashed me."

"That's my great-aunt, right?" I ask, genuinely interested in whether he is referencing the woman who requested an appointment with me, rather than anything he is fretting over.

"You sniveling, arrogant bastard," he fumes. "Stand up and face me if you're going to insult me."

I glance at Phil for some sympathy as I stand up and stare at the grandfather.

"Well?" he glares at me.

"I already insulted you. Now I'm facing you. Do you want me to insult you again so I'm doing both at the same time?"

His right shoulder twitches for several seconds, then his left shoulder, his face contorted with strain through the whole cycle.

"Are you okay?" I ask.

He shrieks in frustration, then breathes heavily into a staring contest with me as his shoulders slacken.

"I want to hit you so bad!" he pants.

"But this place won't let you?"

He appears to try one more time before whirling off as though wearing a cape.

I appreciate the defense provided by this dimension as I watch him walk away, then consider the choice to allow psychological and verbal punches, but not the physical kind. I wonder why the administration decided to make that distinction.

Phil has risen to stand by my side. I nod at him, and when I look back down the dock, the grandfather has disappeared.

"What happens next?" I ask Phil.

"How should I know?"

"Not with that moron. The whole system," I remind him of our conversation before we were interrupted. "The way you imagine it. If this is all a test, what's the prize?"

"Oh, right," he rejoins the discussion. "Another planet, like earth."

I wait to form an answer that might hide my dismay.

"A U-turn?" I surrender.

"No."

"A three-point turn."

"Like earth," he clarifies, "but filled with people who made it to stardust with their dignity intact. Things are back to normal on the new planet, you can't create your own places and situations. There are no projections, just real people, but only people who still had respect for themselves and for others even after they thought they had reached paradise."

"Ah," I see it. "Nice. Is it forever?"

"I haven't thought that far ahead."

"I'm not sure what time is anymore, anyway."

"Me neither."

"I hope you're right about this place."

"Me too."

"For your sake," I clarify. "I hope you're right."

"What about you?"

"I don't think I'm eligible."

"People can change."

"People can," I emphasize the word *people*, and regret it.

"Whatever you did before," Phil does not notice my emphasis, "you seem to be off to a good start here."

"It may not matter."

"I may not be right about how this all works."

"I hope you are," I cannot emphasize this enough.

"For your sake."

I breathe in the scent of pinewood and fresh water.

"You're a good man, Phil."

"Thank you."

I feel like jumping in the lake to complete the cleansing started by the air and water and banishment of the grandfather.

"That great-aunt sounds interesting," I think out loud.

"You've never met her?"

"No..."

I am committing so many slipups with Phil I reflect on whether I am forcing myself to confess to him.

"I mean...yes. But not since I've been here. She requested an appointment, but the thought of her made me uncomfortable. Now I'm thinking that's exactly what I need. She might be able to teach me something about who I was."

"See?" Phil pats me on the back. "You're not the same person."

I appreciate his words of encouragement, but hung up on how I might have to navigate the bureaucracy to make the great-aunt happen.

"Do I have to contact management to re-schedule a denial?"

"I'd send them a text," Phil goes wherever I take our conversation. "Get it in writing. As an old M & O guy, I can only imagine how hard it is to keep track of work orders sent through brainwaves. I used some of the best project management software over my career, and the backlog could still be a nightmare."

"Good call," I take out my phone and type "management" in the contact box, then submit my request.

I move to sit back down on the edge of the dock, but a reply pings before I take a step.

"See?" Phil says. "I'll bet they appreciate you took the time to write it down."

"Request granted," I read aloud.

"You want to see her now?"

"No," I look around. "Not yet."

I follow through on my move, and wind up back on the dock with my feet dangling and my senses full of fresh air and light.

Phil sits next to me.

Chapter Eight

The great-aunt works at a landfill, and she wants to meet me there. I never would have thought all the beautiful, comfortable places I have occupied in the hereafter generate garbage.

"They don't," she says above the clatter of the dump as we walk along a ridgeline overlooking a horizon of rubbish being fought over by hundreds of screeching seagulls and shoved around by a dozen droning bulldozers. "You remember that I worked in waste management, right?"

I nod with no conviction.

"What you probably didn't know is how much I loved it. Nobody understood, so I stopped trying to explain. Even when I relocated here, I wanted to keep doing it, so this is all made-up junk. None of it was ever used for anything else and then discarded. It was garbage from the get-go."

She cups her hands around her mouth.

"Born trash!" she yells down the mound at the nearest bulldozer driver. "Sound like anyone you know, Dano?"

Dano gives her a thumbs-up.

"He didn't hear me," she chuckles.

"Is he a projection?"

"Yup."

"Then who knows?"

She appreciates a good-natured jab at the projections.

"Not that I'm ungrateful," she backtracks. "None of my former employees from the earthly plane want to work here after they make the move. Go figure."

"Odd," I play along.

"They stop by and say hello, I offer them a job, and we laugh."

"That's nice they stop by."

"So what made you change your mind?"

"You know about the denial?"

"The higher-ups don't send you an official message, but at a certain point it's hard not to get the message anyway."

"Sorry."

"I get it," she waves me off. "I wasn't surprised. It was a long shot. But when you reconsidered? Now that was shocking."

She beckons.

"You've seen the great outdoors. Let me show you my office."

We descend the backside of trash mountain to flat land, then walk along a road where the occasional truck full of refuse passes by. Her office is a mobile home next to the gate.

When we enter and she shuts the door, the room feels soundproof for a moment until my ears adjust and I can still hear a faint hum of machinery and big-mouthed birds. The walls are covered in aerial photographs of golf courses, housing developments, and solar farms.

"My babies," she captions the photos. "That's where it all leads."

"These are former landfills?"

"That's right," she beams. "There was a gas energy site too, but that was a little too on-the-nose for me. I like to camouflage. Back when I was kicking it with the living, I never got to do much on that end of the business, not as much as I wanted. Rare, random projects I didn't have any say in. So to be in charge of turning one every year really is paradise, over and over again."

"Congratulations."

"Have a seat," she makes her way to a coffee machine behind her desk. "You want some?"

"No thanks," I sit down in a beaten leather chair facing her desk.

"You seen your grandma yet?" she asks as she pours the watery-looking brew into her mug that says "BOSS" on it.

"Not yet," I can feel the springs in the chair. "I need to work on some things first."

"Work on what?" she takes her seat. "She's your grandma."

"I have questions."

"About what?"

"The kind of person I was."

Any move I make, the springs push me farther in that direction.

"You seen her husband?" she asks. "Excuse me. Your grandpa."

"Yes."

"Well there's your problem."

I squawk like one of the seagulls.

"Too bad he was here first," she says. "I mean, I'm glad Shelly lived longer than him, but for your sake, sorry you had to deal with that right off the bat. Welcome to paradise."

"Did she ask about me?"

"Too many other things to talk about," she shakes her head. "Sorry."

"No," I bounce in the char. "That's fine."

"You didn't spend a lot of time with them."

"That's what I gather."

"What you gather?"

"I mean," I concoct some camouflage of my own to cover up my latest near-giveaway. "I realize now I didn't spend enough time with them. I'm learning all sorts of things after the fact. I didn't know myself very well."

"Hanging out with your grandpa isn't gonna help your education."

"Why do you hate him so much?"

She takes a long sip of coffee and a deep breath.

"Truth be told," she drops in at the end of her exhale, "that whole family pretty much blows."

"Oh yeah?" I am curious, not the least bit defensive.

"He's just the one who convinced her to join it. I warned her, but she was too starry-eyed. Thought she was stepping into a fairytale. I couldn't convince her it was really a viper pit."

She notes how studiously I am taking mental notes.

"You know it, too," she says. "Don't you?"

"A picture is starting to develop."

"What else explains your distance from them?"

"How immersed I was in my work?"

She leans back and howls with laughter.

"Sorry," she overcorrects, hunching forward with a stern expression and grave tone. "Why do you think you were so immersed in your work?"

"I no longer dare to guess."

"There's no guesswork, Devin. You threw yourself into that company because family money paid for it. And the more you could claim to be a workaholic, the more you could claim to be a self-made man and put some distance between yourself and all those advantages you had. That's how your PR department spun it. But your insecurities about how it all started were always going to hover, no matter how far away you ran from those oligarchs. They would always find you."

I am fascinated.

"You're really taking this in stride," she notes.

"It's what I came here for."

She stands up with her mug in hand and steps to the window. She looks through the dusty glass, takes a sip, and grins. I think she might be proud of me. I feel as though I am outside, as a child, the object of her satisfied look, but unaware of it as I play in the garbage.

"What else have you been up to?" she asks, still staring outside.

"Making friends."

"Real people?" she turns away from the window to face me. "Not projections."

"The real deal," I assure her. "Actual former people."

"Anyone I know?"

"Did you ever meet Jane Lamar?"

"Oh no," she sits back down. "She died?"

"Left behind two kids and a husband."

She lowers her head into her hands.

"That's why we're sticking with being friends," I say. "She wants to keep the slate clean so she can assess the situation with them after they arrive. Mainly with the husband, I guess, when it comes to us. But she talks more about her girls."

"Sounds like giving her plenty of space is the right call," Great Aunt comes out from behind her hands.

"Then there's Phil. The greatest guy in the world, who I knew nothing about until I wasn't in the world anymore."

"Explain, please."

"He worked at my company, but in Maintenance and Operations. The blue collar kind, original M & O, not the tech version. I never knew him. His only responsibility was to do his job well, not to impress anyone, least of all me. Now here we are in a place where I don't have any power, so we click."

She offers me the grin she had when looking out the window.

"I feel as though I'm meeting you for the first time," she says.

"Me too," I let the irony fly without fear of detection.

She stands and walks around to the front of her desk, extending her hand in a mock introduction.

"Gladys Booth," she identifies herself.

I stand to shake her hand, but also in honor of finally knowing her name.

"Always a pleasure, Aunt Gladys."

We speak for quite a while longer, she sitting on her desk, me in the old chair with its springs on the verge of punching through the leather. We speak of her family, the people who raised her and her sister, as I gather they were rarely spoken of in the households Devin frequented while he was growing up. We compare the state of the earth when each of us left it, and we compare our reputations, what people would say about each of us when we left the room. Neither of us are surprised by any of the revelations. Maybe Devin himself would be, but not me.

We may not notice the lowering sunlight, but we do see the crew walking past the window, waving good-night to Gladys.

"We should do this again sometime," she says. "Not here, of course. I love my job, but I don't expect you to always hang out with me at the latest dump."

"I don't mind."

"I have a condominium."

"A condo?"

"I know, I know."

"It's the afterlife, Gladys. Come on. Live a little."

"I went big when I first got here, but it felt wrong. I was never home."

"Forever focused on waste."

"It runs through my veins."

Rather than play with her comment about waste running through her veins, I tell her I would love to visit her dinky little condo someday. She slugs me in the arm and gives me a hug.

I ask for directions on the way out.

"You know how it works by now. Head down the road, think about where you're going, and eventually you'll get there."

I follow her directions out of the office and down the lane, but with no particular place to go. I narrow my destination to a couple of options as the dirt road embedded with gravel approaches a bend.

Before I can think of where I would rather be, my orientation specialist and his manager, if those are their job titles, appear around the bend, standing side-by-side in the middle of the road. As I approach, I assume the manager will speak first.

"Mr. Orr."

My assumption is correct.

"Nice of you to say so," I return his nod, then focus on the orientation specialist. "What's up, Melt?"

"Melt?" the manager looks at his underling. "What is he referring to?"

Melt plays dumb for a second before slouching into a confession.

"My nickname," he admits.

"Nicknames. Is that what the floor staff does when we're not watching?"

I cut in.

"You have some news for me?"

"We do," the manager regains his focus. "Shall we go someplace that's not a dirt road leading to a junkyard?"

"The office?" I dread the prospect.

"We don't have to," he counters. "There's a really neat lunch place with outdoor seating where we have staff meetings sometimes."

"Sometimes," Melt mutters.

"Who knew you were so saucy?" the manager reassesses his underling.

"Why are you both here?" I ask.

"I need a witness for this meeting," the manager huffs. "The administration wants to make sure nobody goes rogue. I don't know what they're worried about, with all the fingerprints on this deal. The Re-Entry Committee and the Qualifications Committee couldn't agree on whose jurisdiction your case falls under, so they had to form a mega-committee."

"A mega-committee," I muse.

"They referred to themselves as a board," the manager tries to offer some relief through semantics.

His attempt fails.

"Does this neat lunch place of yours have a full bar?" I ask.

"The mojitos..." Melt makes a euphoric noise and a face to match.

"Sold," I voice my approval, and before we take another step, we are on a terra cotta-colored patio surrounded by hanging flower pots bubbling over with fuchsias and petunias suspended from the beams of a wooden pergola that filters the sunlight, while a collection of potted trees and shrubs line the perimeter to the soothing sounds of a water feature in the corner, the stone face of a lion perpetually spewing a gentle stream of water into the stone tub beneath it.

"We don't have to take an arbitrary trip to get here?" I marvel.

"We have the cheat codes," brags the manager.

He leads us to the one visible table among the contained trees and hanging gardens. We may be the only guests in this oasis. He sends me an expectant look as we all sit down.

"Very nice," I acknowledge.

He is disappointed in my reaction.

"It's one paradise after another around here," I defend my review. "The bar is high."

"Speaking of the bar..." Melt seeks out a server.

The manager fidgets.

"We don't have many points of reference," he excuses his restaurant recommendation. "We're almost always in the office."

"Almost?" Melt cannot resist commenting.

"It's lovely," I step in before they can agitate one another again. "Honestly. I was just teasing you."

A server approaches to take our drink order. Melt and I both offer her thanks at high volume for different reasons. He insists we all order mojitos. The manager and I see no reason to argue with him.

"So..." I preface after the server leaves. "What's the verdict?"

"Well..." the manager prefaces back. "They're prepared to offer a mulligan."

"Really?" I am not sure how to feel.

"There are concerns about how your condition may affect the process, namely with regard to how permanent Devin's imprint is on you, but eventually the committee concluded that any remnants of Devin will be overwhelmed by the volume of new stimuli and memories developed from birth in your new body."

"A body of my own?"

"You'll be a real boy."

"Or girl," reminds Melt.

"You'll be an original," the manager summarizes.

"And they're not worried if someone, something, like me can actually become human?"

"You've made it this far," the manager says. "That was good enough for them."

"Wow," I use a word I tried not to use too often on earth as I sit back and parse the news.

Our server returns with the drinks and distributes them. Each thud of a glass landing on the table sends me deeper into thought. On the first beat I think of Aunt Gladys, on the second I think of Phil, and on the third knock I think of Jane.

The server asks if we are ready to order, at least I assume she asks. I do not hear any voices until Melt asks me what I would like, and I snap out of my countdown to find them all staring at me. I tell her I will have what Melt is having.

"Good choice," she says, whatever that choice may be.

"Is she a projection?" I ask after she leaves. "Or one of you?"

"A projection," the manager answers.

I nod and sink back into the memories I have made with the people I have met since I arrived.

"You don't have to decide right away," the manager reads my consternation. "You've been doing a great job playing the part."

"It's not much of a decision," I say.

"Oh?" the manager peps up.

"I haven't been around long enough to choose stardust. It's mulligan all the way."

The manager and Melt exchange a moment of communion. Melt reaches for his mojito. The manager reaches for a reminder.

"Your life will be the farthest thing from what it was the first time," he says.

"I know."

"I mean," Melt is inspired by the first sip of his drink, "there's a small chance it will be something vaguely similar."

"A microscopic chance," the manager looks as though he wants to pull the straw from Melt's mouth.

"I won't know the difference," I say to both of them and neither of them. "It will all to be new to me."

"We assume," the manager reiterates. "If instead you retain more of Devin's imprint than the board anticipated, a life of scarcity and desperation would be made that much more difficult."

"Do you want me to go stardust instead?"

"Of course not. The choice is yours."

"Is it? Because it sounds like the board is quite proud of themselves for offering a mulligan, but you're out here by the fountain under the flower pots sabotaging the deal."

"I'm following their orders. They knew you would leap at the chance for more life, but wanted to make sure you understood it comes with certain problems."

"The only problem is leaving behind the friends I've made," I clear up the fog they had trouble seeing me through. "I'm going to miss them."

The manager and Melt register more sympathy than I thought them capable of, even with Melt sucking on a straw, which might actually enhance his warmth.

"How much time do I have before I need to go through with it?"

"I can buy you the equivalent of one day on earth."

"I'd like to say some good-byes."

The manager looks at me sideways.

"Without actually saying good bye, of course."

He still looks skeptical.

"You said I've been doing a great job of playing along."

"Make sure you keep it up," he says. "Otherwise the deal is off."

I hold up my hands in either surrender or assurance, when something occurs to me.

"What happens between when I'm gone and when Devin arrives?"

"They're going with a projection of him."

"More like a projection of me."

"Okay."

"A clone of a clone," I try to make it sound as ridiculous as possible.

Melt sees my point and needs to swallow his current sip earlier than he had planned.

"What are you getting at?" the manager is not so amused. "That you should be allowed to stay until Devin gets here?"

"I guess so," I realize. "Yeah. That's exactly what I'm getting at. A projection can't do what I do. It can't sustain my relationships."

"You're probably right. But ultimately, that will be Devin's problem, not yours."

"It's not just about him and me. It's about the other people, too. The people we're involved with."

The manager sits back and exhales. He looks over at Melt, who shrugs, his interest having returned to his mojito.

"You know very well what you're suggesting isn't possible."

"I don't know that very well. I don't know that at all. If I knew that, I wouldn't be suggesting otherwise."

"Well," he works hard to stay calm. "Then I hate to break the news to you—"

"Those relationships are mine!" I interrupt. "He broke them, he ignored them, and I fixed them!"

"He broke more than that," the manager is done entertaining my argument. "Your original, your first edition, whatever he is, messed with the fabric of the universe enough, and it stops here."

"I had nothing to do with it," I throw up one last defense, knowing I am about to lose.

"But you are a product of him," he reasons as though writing out an equation. "And he is a menace to the cosmos."

Melt finishes his drink with a long, loud slurp of the straw, using it to vacuum the bottom of the glass.

"He did clone himself," Melt slurs to a conclusion. "What kind of a man clones himself?"

He slaps his empty tumbler onto the table, and it feels like a gavel being hammered by a judge.

I feel as chastened as Devin might be if he was here, probably more so.

Very likely more so.

We sit in silence for the final minute before our food arrives, and when it does, that gives us an excuse to remain silent even longer while we eat, aside from Melt ordering another mojito.

When I finish, I wait for them to finish, and when they have, I ask the manager for confirmation.

"One day?"

He nods.

I stand up and walk out.

Right before I leave the overgrown patio behind, I hear the manager ask his underling for clarification.

"Why is your name Melt?"

Chapter Nine

The condominium complex Gladys created is a perfect rendition of a home for people who are never home. We stand by the community pool drinking cans of beer. We are the only ones there, perhaps the only ones ever to stand next to the pool, much less swim in it. Beer tastes good after the only sip I could muster of Melt's favorite too-sweet mojito.

"Any other people live here?" I ask.

"Projections of them. The kind of people who come and go at odd times, just like they would on earth. Gig workers, contractors, bartenders, graveyard shifts—"

"Graveyard shifts," I force a joke onto the line.

Gladys offers me a fist bump.

I take her up on it.

"I didn't expect to hear from you so soon," she says after we tap our knuckles.

The manager is right. Whatever happens after I leave is Devin's problem. If the projection of me, of the clone he designed, or if Devin himself someday ruins every relationship forged during my brief stay in the afterlife, I will never know. But these relationships are my legacy, the only accomplishment I can claim for however long I existed in either world. Devin will learn what came before him when he finally arrives, and I want him to be impressed to the point of being ashamed. He will know what I created turned out better than anything he could have imagined.

"You brought a lot out of me," I tell Great Aunt Gladys. "I wish I gave you that chance before, when life was in real time."

"My goodness," she hides behind a sip from her can. "Thank you."

"See?" I capitalize on the moment. "Getting things out in the open, confronting life, the afterlife, it can be uncomfortable."

"I don't mind honesty," she emerges from her mouthful. "Compliments make me edgy."

"I like compliments," I go full Devin. "I may be in love with them. Even if they're not sincere. It's an unhealthy relationship."

"You seem willing to work on it."

"I'm trying," I lay the foundation for my replacement. "But if I seem strange, or you feel like I'm avoiding you, even when I'm spending time with you, it just means I'm still opening the gift you gave me."

"How long do you think you'll be opening that gift?"

I revel in her bluntness.

"Days? Weeks?" she piles on. "Eternity?"

"Long enough so you might not want to hang out with me anymore," I nudge my beer in her direction for a down-low toast. "But I hope you do."

She glances down at the can, then looks back up and forward before agreeing to a gentle tap.

I change the subject to how her latest project is coming along, what transformation she is summoning from an island of glut. Garbage heap to golf course? Trash pile to tract homes?

While she provides her update, some neighbors start to appear, making their way to the pool area one at a time. I suspect she may be conjuring them, building a party to distract us both. Some bring more beer, others bring snacks. As the disturbance builds, one of them wheels in a grill, which inspires a few to rush back to their units and return with chicken breasts and hamburger patties. Spices and sauces appear, perhaps delivered by projections I do not notice, but just as likely imagined into existence.

Two half-eaten burgers and umpteen beers later, after I cannonball fully-clothed into the pool, I wonder as I pause underwater if I may have contributed to this party, if it was a joint effort between me and the great-aunt neither I nor Devin ever really had. I resurface and look at her. She is busy talking to a neighbor, but I am more convinced than before that not only did we throw this party together, she knows precisely why we are throwing it, right down to what I really am.

The prospect is exhilarating. I feel as though I could swim to my next stop.

I give it a try.

I dive back under, breast stroking and kicking my way to the bottom of the pool, but never reach it.

The pool light disappears. The water turns dark. I cannot hold my breath any longer. I reverse course and swim upward. The water tastes salty. I break the surface, gasping for air.

As I tread water and get used to breathing again, I bob in time to the undulating water. I hear a small wave crest behind me, turn to catch its approach, and duck under. I rise after it passes, keep an eye on its path, and spot lights on the shore. The lights multiply. They are coming from a resort. I swim toward it.

No one notices or cares that I am soaking wet. The front desk checks me in as though I am wearing a freshly-pressed suit. A concierge catches up to me as I approach the elevators and says there is a change of clothes in my room. I thank him and when he asks if there is anything else he can do, I make a breakfast reservation for the following morning. He asks if I will be dining alone, and I tell him my friend Phil will be joining me.

I dream of trying to keep my head above the water in rough, open seas, which would not be surprising but for the fact it is the first time I have dreamed in the afterlife. I guess we have little reason to imagine anything while we are asleep when every waking moment is a dream, and when the definition of being awake is unsettled.

I arrive at this conclusion while waiting for Phil at a table by the pool. I am sitting at this table because my last meeting next to a pool went so well, I dare say swimmingly, and I am willing to believe whatever may foretell a productive farewell.

Of the projections sitting poolside, I note a man smoking a cigarette. When Phil approaches and apologizes for being late, which I assure him he is not because I arrived early, I direct us further away from the subject of who is late and who is early by pointing out the smoker.

"Oh, yeah," he glances at him. "I did that."

"You put the projection of a man smoking there?"

"Yes."

"I didn't know we could add things to other people's simulations."

"It's pretty limited. You've probably done it and didn't know."

I think of the condiments for the burger that appeared at the condo pool party.

"I probably have," I realize.

We order coffee from a server who tells us we can visit the buffet anytime. We thank him for the information, but reach an unspoken agreement to wait until after we have our coffee to fetch breakfast.

"Why a smoker?" I ask after the server walks away.

"I plant one every so often to remind me how stupid it would be to smoke here."

"You used to smoke?"

"A lot," he stresses the amount. "On earth."

"I imagine it's not as bad for you here."

"It isn't bad for you at all," he verifies. "But why get away with it when it's just as easy to stop?"

I consider asking him if he thought of that before or after he formulated his hypothesis on the afterlife as a test, but instead lean back and appreciate his idea and his friendship while I look at the ocean.

"I don't think I ever had a really good friend on earth," I cast my words out to sea.

"You think it was because of your position?" he asks.

"In part."

"Would you have had more friends if you were the same kind of person, but without the position?"

His question is fair, as his questions tend to be, which is bad news for what I want to say next. I want to tell him I am so unaccustomed to friendship that if I come across as eccentric in the days to come, rest assured the fault is mine, not his.

Now as I run the line in my head, it sounds indulgent. Phil would not mind. He would let me get away with it, like Aunt Gladys when I ran something similar by her, but as with smoking, not doing it is as easy as indulging in it. I decide to instead play around in shallow waters.

"It's a perfectly good excuse," I conclude with regard to my earthly power undermining my friendships. "Let me cling to it."

The server arrives with our coffee, offering a chance to jump off my train of thought. I zero in on the present. The coffee makes me think of other stimulants, including cigarettes, so I ask Phil if he tried to quit smoking, which he did, and about the various ways he tried, which were many.

As Phil describes all the different methods, I think "to hell with Devin" and decide to relegate him to an afterlife of awkward encounters with people who once thought they liked him, even loved him, but who wonder where his spark went, and as preposterous as it may sound, if he is even the same person they used to know.

But this is Phil. He is fine with anyone for who they are. Devin will be no exception.

"I understand you showed up wet," Phil interrupts my mental flattery of him, as though he knows and wants to change the subject. "Epic move."

"One of the employees told you?"

"It's the talk of the resort."

"I didn't think projections notice much of anything."

"Maybe they just don't want us to feel self-conscious while we live out our fantasies."

Phil even sticks up for projections. He and the one based on me will get along fine. Devin might just keep it around after he arrives. He has a history with clones, after all. If only the administration lets him.

"More like we don't want them to make us feel self-conscious," I add a corollary to his proposition about the projections.

We take a trip to the buffet and back and I explain to Phil why I checked in wet.

"You swam here?"

"Like I said, I came up just outside the surf. It was a very afterlife version of swimming to Hawaii."

"The length isn't the point. That's an impressive manipulation for someone who hasn't been here long. From a pool to the Pacific Ocean. You're already an afterlife alpha dog."

I delight in the term, but Phil is being earnest.

"We should think of a cool way to head back to the mainland together," he is determined to capitalize on my supposed powers.

"Maybe a boat," I suggest.

"A speedboat," he chomps on a piece of bacon. "Better yet, two speedboats. Let's race."

"Or hang gliders."

"A hang glider race," he continues to take me seriously.

"How about a hang glider versus a speedboat?"

"Which one do you want?"

I laugh my way into the pile of scrambled eggs on my plate.

"I mean it," he says.

"I know you do," I eat to help turn down the expectations. "But you're putting an awful lot of faith in my abilities."

"Mine and yours combined," he waves his fork back and forth between us. "I've been doing this for a while. I didn't think you'd be ready so soon."

"Ready?"

"Ready to take full advantage of what we can do here."

"So you don't really like to hang out and talk?"

"I like that, sure. But come on. You jumped into a pool and came out in the surf along the beach at Maui. Don't you want to ride home on a jet ski surrounded by dolphins?"

I put my fork down.

When we reach the beach, we spot the pod of dolphins circling beyond the waves.

Their backs and dorsal fins reflect the light, while the spray they exhale catches it.

The water temperature is warmer than the real Pacific, so we wade right into the shallows still dressed for breakfast, guiding the jet skis the concierge reserved for us until the sandy floor gives way beneath us. When we jump on them and accelerate over the waves to meet the pod, the dolphins likewise spring into another gear, moving faster, breaching higher, and falling in line around us as we head into the open water. Some of them take the lead, some stick by our side, others spin beneath us. I focus on one of them weaving around his colleagues in front, and as he falls back to Phil's side, Phil and I make eye contact and exchange a small smile for a moment to confirm that this is happening, and it is fantastic.

In true afterlife fashion, we spot the mainland in fifteen minutes, and aim for a town teeming with tourists and gift shops where we can pick up a change of clothes. We drag the jet skis onto the narrow, wet sandy shore and walk up the weather-beaten stairs that scale the cliffs upon which the town is perched. Phil half-jokes we should have tried to submerge and reemerge in a pool at a theme park where a dolphin show was taking place so we could break the surface as the big finish, but conjuring up a stadium full of spectators was probably more than we could manage after an exhilarating but exhausting ride, plus it strikes us as exploitative. The pod was kind enough to escort us home. No need to put them on display. He settles for being able to join me this time while walking wet in public. We slosh to a shop and discover most of the clothes feature the name of the town.

"Monterey?" I ask Phil.

"Yeah," he says while sifting through a rack of fleece vests.

"Have you ever been to Monterey?"

"A couple of times."

"Did you not pay attention when you were there?"

"It's been a while," he stops sifting. "I remember some nice restaurants and walking by the water. You've seen one seaside town, you've seen them all."

"Laguna Beach does not look like Monterey."

"Ooh," he implies pompousness. "Excuse me."

"Well, Joe Lunch Bucket, this town you designed looks a lot more like Laguna than Monterey."

"I guess hanging around you is bringing out my inner snob."

I celebrate in stillness that before I have to go, we reached a point where we can go hard at poking fun at each other. I choose a Monterey sweatshirt to commemorate the moment.

We part as though riding with dolphins across the simulated Pacific was no more remarkable than playing softball on a Sunday afternoon. When we say good bye, I consider embracing him, but lay off, because a simple good bye is the most fitting way to put our friendship to rest.

I do watch him walk away longer than a friend would under normal circumstances. I feel like a rescue animal being released back into its natural habitat. I have enjoyed my time here, bonded with those who saved me, but this is not my world. Several seconds of sentimentality, then the natural order pulls us back into our parts that we play.

I have waited to see if Jane is free because I should leave her alone. I contact her expecting her to be busy, but hoping she can make it.

She can.

She asks where, and the first place I think of is the park where we met before our trip to Las Vegas. The bookstore is too full of our past.

The park is neutral, and I would like to experience it without Devin's grandfather ambushing me with silent street magic.

Getting there gives me pause. I could use the Aunt Gladys method and start walking the streets of Monterey-by-Phil while thinking of the park, or take my recent flair for a spin and ride a rental bike off the end of a pier, but wonder if maybe since my time is almost up, the management is willing to surrender the cheat codes and let me beam directly to the park bench, if beaming is the right term.

I thank them out loud as I see Jane approaching while I rise from a park bench to greet her.

"How was Monterey?" she acknowledges my sweatshirt.

"Not like I remember it."

She blesses me with a peck on the cheek.

"I'm glad you called," she says. "I was afraid maybe Vegas scared you off."

"Vegas didn't scare me off. You, on the other hand…"

She gives me a follow-up hug. I am so glad I get to see her.

"Plus I got this weird message," she tells me as we sit down.

"Oh yeah?" I settle in for a conversation.

"Another one about making an appointment with you," she is not ready to settle. "Like when you arrived."

I sigh as if on the phone with a customer service center that has put me on hold yet again while troubleshooting yet another problem with my account, the latest hiccup being the announcement of a projection that is supposed to take over for me without anyone knowing.

"One thing after another," I narrate my exasperation with a typical phrase intended to keep me from spilling the glitch. "Since the day I arrived."

"Maybe they do this to every tech mogul who passes through. Purgatory for what they did to their customers."

"My company wouldn't survive if I treated customers this way."

"Damn government workers," she mocks. "Lifelong bureaucrats with their cradle-to-grave job security."

"Is that supposed to be me?" I inquire after her impersonation.

"More of a generic guy like you."

"Doesn't make the point any less true," I grouse.

Her jab having landed, she sits back to watch the projections enjoy a day in the park. In particular, a pair of little girls squealing by, one chasing the other, catches her eye. I may have had something to do with that.

"I have a plan," she says.

"Spill it."

"I finally managed to look at some photos of the girls."

"Oh yeah?"

"We were at an art festival they put on in our town every year. It was designed for local artists to display their work in the park, but we'd go for the activities. There were a bunch of different booths where the kids could paint and do crafts. One was a group painting project. Each kid contributes to this larger beautiful mess on a big piece of wood that's eventually mounted on a couple of posts and planted in one of the landscaping borders around one of the parking lots. There are individual projects, too. But I remember the big group blobs the most, since they stick around the longest. Most of the smaller works get tossed the minute everyone gets home. Some may last a little longer, or years, depending on how much the parents are willing to hoard. Those big pieces, though, become part of the town. I liked looking at the ones from way before we ever moved there, much less had kids. The first piece in the collection is from 1972. Some of the adults who painted on it when they were kids are still in town. I knew a couple of them when I was still around. I would stare at the swirls and streaks from way back when and wonder which marks were made by kids who moved away when they grew up, which ones stayed, what they ended up doing with their lives, which ones lost their lives before they should have. I thought about those big pieces while my girls contributed their dollops. My oldest wanted to make hers look good. She painted a mouse. I think that's what it was. She has to work so much harder than the other kids. I assumed it was a mouse when I told her it looked great."

"Well, if she didn't correct you…"

"I didn't say 'cute mouse'. I knew better. I just said it looked great."

"You really are a good mother."

"Or at least a smart one. When they were done, they played in the fountain on the other end of the park with a bunch of other kids. It's one of those fountains that's programmed to squirt water from different places at different times, choreographed, like a miniature version of the dancing waters outside the Bellagio in Las Vegas. That's how my youngest put it. When we saw the dog show, we passed by that fountain and she made the connection, not me. I'm borrowing her comparison. Everything comes naturally to her. They're very different girls. About all they have in common is they look alike. Anyway, all the kids scream like that fountain is the most terrifying and hilarious thing they've ever experienced. And they never seem to figure out the pattern of the water. Maybe they don't want to. I watched them and thought of the big pieces of art made by all those children who passed through the park. I loved that my kids were becoming a part of that collection, that tradition. I loved that day. It was the kind of day when you say something like 'I wish this day could last forever.'"

The one projection of a girl catches the other projection of a girl, who shrieks at being caught. For a moment joy hangs in the balance, dependent upon whether it was a shriek of anguish or glee. Joy wins. The girl takes her turn being the chaser. Jane smiles as she watches them reverse their roles.

"So your plan is to see if you really can make that day last forever," I conclude.

"I'm going to relive it on a loop," she confirms. "See how many days in a row we can stand it."

"We?"

"I know. The girls will be projections. They won't get tired of it. I'm the one inviting boredom. And when boredom comes, I'm going to relive that day as a kid. I haven't tried adjusting my age since I've been here. I was happy with my age when I died. But I want to do it when I can't stand that day any longer as an adult, and see if being a kid keeps it alive. I'm going to paint with them and run around screaming in the fountain with them, and see how much kids really do live in the moment. I told you how much I've agonized over meeting my girls when they're older, and whether I should ask them to be children again when they get here. I finally realized I might be the one who needs to go backward."

She will not actually be a kid. She knows that. No need for me to tell her. But I am not sure what else to say, and she responds to my silence.

"I'm sorry for getting morbid again," she says. "I vowed not to do that this time. My plan sounded a lot more funny and uplifting when I rehearsed it in my head. I mean, being a kid again. Wee! Sounds like something stitched on a kitchen towel."

"You have nothing to apologize for. I can listen to you talk about anything."

"That's nice of you to say."

"It's true," I know I need to stop there, and do, for a second, before hearing myself continue. "Whatever our problems may have been, loving you was not one of them."

She tangles up in a bunch of emotions, none of them happiness.

I feel like a needy clone who does not understand human emotion. I look around for a diversion and spot some food trucks parked along the perimeter of the promenade.

"Would you like some ice cream?" I ask. "Or a taco?"

She sees what I am doing.

"Maybe a snack," she agrees to my scheme and scans the trucks. "Kettle corn sounds good."

"Kettle corn sounds great," I enthuse. "I'll be right back."

"Thank you," she says, and her gratitude has nothing to do with kettle corn.

I may not have much time before my memories of Jane are lost, but I still try to make the last twenty seconds go away by distracting myself with reasons for why we eat in the afterlife. Pleasure is the easy answer, but I think community may loom larger, something to do while talking to someone. I have not eaten alone in the afterlife, and cannot imagine why anyone would.

"Awesome," the kettle corn vendor says as he scoops the contents into a bag. "Man, you are absolutely crushing it."

I exit my meditation on the point of food in the afterworld to look at him and ask him what on earth he is talking about and find the earth hurtling toward me, earth in the form of Devin, holding the bag, grinning at himself, at his own reflection, at me.

"You were programmed to be charming," my clone fills the dead air between us. "But this is way beyond expectations."

"I still have a few more hours," I regain my voice.

"Not anymore."

"Management can eat it," I bark. "They botched your release enough already with that stupid announcement. They owe me that much."

I grab the bag, but he does not let it go.

"The announcement was legit," he says. "I'm not your clone."

He releases his grip.

"You're my clone," he lets me have it.

I hold the bag as though it is holding me up.

"Devin?"

"Scuba diving accident," he answers the look on my face.

"What is it with this park?" I look around as if the answer might be carved into a hedge.

"We were celebrating the sale of the company."

"You sold the company?"

"We were about to…"

A teenaged projection gets in line behind me. Devin shoos him away.

"We're out of whatever it is I sell," he says.

"Kettle corn," I cue him.

"We're out of that," he keeps shooing.

The projection shrugs and shuffles off.

"Like it matters if these dips hear us, right?" Devin cracks.

I wait on the rest of the story.

"Anyway," he picks it up, "we hadn't signed the contracts yet. We were going to do that after the trip, after the lawyers did their thing. And then, whoops!"

"What happened?"

"Not sure. I wasn't conscious for most of it. But the team needs me for the signing ceremony, otherwise the deal might fall through. And by me, I mean you, of course."

"Of course?"

"We didn't delete you at the launch. Just put you on ice, so to speak. Actually, I mean that literally. Well, not an actual tub of ice, or a freezer. More of a Walt Disney, Ted Williams kind of situation."

I am more speechless than when I first saw him.

"Look," he says. "I appreciate how much this is to take in, but we're in the ultimate crunch time here. You could be revived any minute now."

I turn to look at Jane. She is still sitting on the bench contemplating the projections passing by.

"Okay," I concede. "I'll be right back."

Devin comes around from behind the cart and blocks my way.

"Don't bother," he tells me.

"I need to say good bye."

"We need to go to the office."

"The manager's office?"

"The same one you've been dealing with," he considers this good news. "They figured it would help move things along."

"This is between you and them. You're the one who busted their system."

I try to brush past him, but he clutches my shoulder.

"Don't worry about her, Doc."

"Doc?"

"D.O.C.," he spells it out as an acronym. "Devin Orr Clone."

"Is that what you called me behind my back."

"Everything took place behind your back."

"Shouldn't you get back behind the cart?" I roll my shoulder out from under his grip. "She might see us standing together."

"She won't look over."

"How do you know?"

"Because this is my world now, Doc."

I study him.

"You are so much worse than I imagined," I conclude.

"I'm not posturing," he says. "That is a fact. I am the rightful owner of this simulation. Your time is up. You've done some beautiful work here. You're a stud, a player. But you don't know her like I know her, and my idea of paradise does not include her."

I look at Jane, willing her to look at me, fighting for eye contact one last time.

"What's the old breakup line?" Devin narrates my effort. "It's not you, it's me."

I feel his hand on my shoulder again. I swat it away and spin around, the bag bursting into a cascade of popped corn.

"Get your hands off me!"

He is standing in the office.

So am I.

The park is gone.

And with it, Jane.

"Hello, Mr. Orr."

I turn to see the manager. He is sitting behind a desk. We are in his private office.

"Where is Melt?" I ask.

"Out on the floor, in his cubicle, introducing someone to what comes next."

I feel myself breathe. I am calm, but not relaxed.

"Lucky them," I say.

I might whisper it, I might not even say it out loud, but I mean it.

Chapter Ten

Devin disguises his cruelty as a sense of humor.

"It's just another case of a guy going out for a bag of corn nuts and never coming back," he flops on a couch next to the closed door and stretches his arms along the top of the backrest, as if his sarcasm is the last word on the matter.

"It was kettle corn," I lower myself into a chair by the manager's desk, still holding the empty bag, which is now a torn piece of rumpled paper. I stare at it, something that survived my time spent as someone.

The only other something besides my Monterey sweatshirt. I look down at the name ironed across the front as a place to aspire to, a kind of happiness that might be possible again.

"I still can't get over how amazing you turned out," Devin compliments me as if I am an engraved wrist watch or a hand-stitched leather briefcase. "Your attention to detail is incredible. A world-class schmooze depends on details about the people you're schmoozing."

I start to emerge from my haze of disappointment on a platform of anger.

"I wasn't schmoozing anyone here. And it's not that hard to remember I ordered kettle corn two minutes ago."

"But the moves. The way you read Jane like source code. If things weren't so time sensitive, I could follow you around for days and watch you work on everyone else."

"Why isn't there a hell?" I ask the manager. "I know there isn't one because I would have ended up there since you thought I was him. But can you make one? Can he go there?"

"We need to focus," the manager says. "Like Devin says, we don't have much time."

"Devin?" I stand up. "So he's Devin. Does that mean you're calling me Doc, too?"

"I don't know what you're talking about, Mr. Orr."

"And I don't trust anything that comes out of your mouth. Or whatever that thing is on your face. If that's even a face. What are you?"

Devin snickers.

The manager and I both glare at him.

"It's a fair question," he defends his snicker.

"I know what you are," I walk toward the couch he has claimed for himself with the spread of his arms and legs. "You're one of those guys who always lands on their feet. You don't always win, but you never really lose. And it has nothing to do with talent."

"Bad clone," he wags his finger at me like I am his pet. "Bad clone."

I try to lunge at him, but the rules of the afterlife hold me back.

"You know how it is here, Doc," he grins. "I'm a quick study, too. You're a spectacular recipe, but the cloners had some good ingredients to work with."

Since I cannot grab him, I wad the rumpled paper into a ball and see if I am able to throw it at him. I am. It hits him in the chest and tumbles to the floor.

I turn to the manager again.

"Build a hell," I implore him. "Open a franchise for this swaggering gob of entitlement, see how it goes, then take it from there."

"They've had worse candidates than me," Devin acknowledges his own awfulness and dismisses it all at once.

"We've had more obvious candidates," the manager corrects him with enough sincerity to offend Devin and amuse me.

"Be that as it may," Devin brandishes a cliché to sweep away the insult before moving on. "You're about to become a very wealthy earthling thanks to me."

I take a deep breath as if to say something, but say nothing.

"You're welcome," he prods.

"Can I still take the mulligan?" I ask the manager while still staring at Devin.

I hear an uneasy grunt come from the manager.

"You're kidding," I give him my full attention.

"It would be terribly risky."

"How so?"

"We're not sure, but…"

"Stop there," I aim my hands at him as though trying to fire lightning bolts from my fingertips. "I'm so tired of hearing that from you. 'We're not sure'. 'We don't know'. You're all-powerful, all-knowing lords of the afterlife and you never have any answers. I might as well be at a free clinic in a rundown city on earth."

"I'm sorry, but every move you make is unprecedented," the manager defends his team. "People are not supposed to be able to go back and forth between here and there."

"He's not a person," Devin butts in without getting up.

"I'm more of a person than you ever were," I face him.

"Technically not possible."

"Technically," I grant him. "But what is a person?"

"Oh, boy," the manager murmurs.

"Have I not developed deep human relationships during my stay? Is that not the essence of being human? Does that not count for anything here?"

"It's not about what we're doing here," the manager continues to run damage control from his desk. "It's what they're doing over there. They really have disrupted the filament of the universe."

"I know I should be ashamed," Devin preens. "But I confess to feeling quite giddy."

The manager and I look at each other rather than at him.

"You'll look into that hell proposal?" I ask the manager.

"I'll put it on the agenda of our next meeting."

Devin laughs.

"I have little to no concept of humor," the manager reminds him.

"Nor the ability to tell a human from a clone," Devin retaliates.

"That's not my department."

"All right, all right," I retrace our footsteps. "So what's the problem with the mulligan?"

"Uncharted territory," the manager regains his mild manner. "The effect on the body and mind you'd be born into could be catastrophic. If we grant you the mulligan, and your essence is whisked away while you're still in the womb, which is practically guaranteed to happen if you're as close to being revived as Devin claims, then a million paths open up, nearly all of them bad."

"While on the other hand," Devin interjects, "you can keep that essence where it is and wake up from a deep freeze filthy rich."

"And polish your legacy?"

"If you want to," he pretends not to care.

I stare at the wall hoping for a third option.

"You brought me here to tell me I don't have a choice," I address neither of them in particular.

"We thought it best you hear about each option from its source," the manager says.

"Like a little devil on one shoulder," Devin seizes a classic illustration but realizes the image will not hold. "And...another little devil on your other shoulder."

"You're not making yourself the little angel in that chestnut?" I am surprised.

"That was the idea," he admits. "But there's one more thing I need to tell you that wouldn't make it fly. Ha! Fly."

"What?"

"The angel won't fly."

"I get it," I acknowledge before prompting him. "The other thing you need to tell me...?"

Devin appears humble for the first time in the ten minutes total I have interacted with him on earth and in the afterlife. He folds himself into less space on the couch.

"It may not have been a scuba diving accident," he looks down and away.

"You can't remember if you were scuba diving?"

"No, that's not what I mean."

"Maybe you were you on safari, attacked by hyenas."

"I mean emphasis on the word 'accident,'" he stalls before continuing. "I think, it's possible, maybe, it was on purpose."

"Murdered?" I force the word on him.

Devin glances at the door as though paranoid someone may have their ear pressed against it.

"You think you may have been murdered?" I spread more words onto the question.

"Yes," the manager answers for him. "He thinks he may have been murdered."

"So what does that have to do with me?" I ask the manager. "Aside from confirming my suspicions about his character?"

"If it's true," Devin speaks for himself, "they might try to screw us. Screw you. And might I say 'screw you' for that last crack about my character. That's not their motive."

"It's about money," I assume.

"And my team," he grumbles. "Those backstabbing, succubus scum who want to take my money. I may as well have been attacked by hyenas on safari."

"You think they're going to redraw the contracts before bringing me back to sign them," I presume.

"I am positive they're going to do that, even if it was an accident."

"How will I know?"

Devin's eyes double in size.

"You're going back?" he prepares to celebrate.

I am loathe to feed his joy, but have little choice. Rather than say yes, I repeat the question.

"How will I know if I'm getting screwed?"

"Yes!" Devin raises his arms in the air and springs up from the couch, then shifts gears into a spasm of fist pumps and leg kicks.

I sit on the manager's desk and we watch the one-man party play out.

"There is a bright side to going back and pretending to be him that has nothing to do with money," the manager says as we watch Devin wind down.

"What's that?" I ask, fascinated by Devin's stamina for gloating.

"You'll be able to remember the friends you made here."

I look back at him and we appreciate one another for a moment. Devin claps his hands and cuts it short.

"Okay!" he moves from clapping his hands to rubbing them. "Let's do this."

He approaches me like a coach who has a player he is eager to put in the game.

"You were designed to raise money, not manage it," he puts his hands together and aims them at me, as if he was about to pray but decided lecturing me was more important. "So I won't overwhelm you with the details of the sale."

"Thanks," I deadpan.

"All you need to know is one figure," he pronounces. "Sixty-five percent."

"Sixty-five percent," I repeat. "Of what? What does that mean?"

"They'll know what it means. And you knowing it will absolutely freak them out. Which is funny and I wish I could be there to see the looks on their faces, but freaking them out is also important. You want them scared. Not just so they don't give you a raw deal, but so they don't get rid of you after it's done."

"I hadn't thought of that," I admit.

"You're the charming one," he reminds me. "I'm the ruthless one."

"So play up the otherworldly angle," I corroborate the plan. "Let them know I've been to the beyond and back."

"Well..." the manager chimes in.

"Within reason," I acknowledge his concern.

"Less is more," Devin preps me for the performance. "If you say too much, they have grounds to check you into a psychiatric ward. But drop a little bit of knowledge on them, they might check themselves in."

"And don't let them know how I know what I know," I build on the strategy.

"Be an enigma," Devin encourages the idea.

"Please," the manager encourages it even more. "Be an extremely enigmatic one."

"Okay, then," I swing my arms as if preparing to dive into a pool. "I guess we're good to go."

Devin applauds.

The manager rises from behind his desk and comes around to shake my hand.

"I'm sorry we weren't ready for you," he says as we pump our clasped hands. "We really are an efficient organization under normal circumstances."

"I understand," I say as we stop the pump and release our grip. "I'm sorry I was such a difficult customer."

"We've learned a lot from you," he pats me on the back.

I nod for a few seconds.

"Thank you," I add.

We stand there for a few more seconds.

"You're welcome," he decides to say.

I put my hands in my pants pockets.

The manager fastens his hands behind his back.

Devin crosses his arms.

"Any idea how long it might take them to unthaw me?" I ask Devin.

"That's not really how it works," he answers. "It's not like taking something out of a freezer. It's much faster."

"How fast?" I press him.

"Hours," he replies. "They have logistical issues that might take extra time to iron out, mostly concerning my body, not yours. But they probably already made the changes to the business purchase agreement and scaled back the PR blitz. And swearing a blood oath to keep their secret shouldn't take long, depending on how sharp a knife those venal little mutineers use to conduct the ceremony."

"Well," I consider the assessment of Aunt Gladys and whether to share it. "That's who you end up with when you bury yourself in work and don't make any real friends."

Sharing appears to have inflicted genuine hurt onto Devin, or inspired a believable performance.

"I'm trying to help you here," he sets sail on a guilt trip. "And you have to go there?"

"Sorry," I concede my timing may be off.

"I thought we reached an understanding," he carries on. "We had a real moment happening."

"Is there anything you don't overdo?" I retract my concession.

"If there was, you wouldn't exist."

"Rather than going back to taking shots at each other," the manager steps in. "Maybe we can just get back to being uncomfortable."

We retreat to our corners while standing in place.

I revisit Devin's reply to my question about time.

"So you're not sure how long this might take."

"Not down to the minute or anything," he confirms. "No."

The three of us relapse into our clumsy triangle of silence, as the manager wished.

I think of what I might do with the mysterious amount of time I have before re-entry. My ideal would be to gather Gladys, Phil, and Jane all together in one place, someplace peaceful, maybe the pool area by the condo, or the bar with the big open window in my version of Maui, or the park where I left Jane, where I could listen to them talk to each other and learn as much as possible about them and about people in general before I am sucked back to earth. But I would not want to disappear in front of them. Not because I assume any heartbreak on their part, but for the confusion it would cause. I have disrupted their afterlives enough already. I need to leave them alone.

"I think I'll go to my house," I say. "The house I thought up, and take a nap. Maybe I'll wake up on earth, unfrozen and rich."

"Make sure it's the negotiated amount of rich," Devin reminds me as I make my way to the door.

"I will," I turn to look at the two of them as I stand at the threshold.

Having them as the last faces I see makes leaving easier. I suppress a chuckle until I close the door behind me.

Before I let go of my laugh, the floor drops out from under me and everything inside my body is punched upward.

I feel as though I am falling toward maximum velocity, but the world around me is not speeding past. What I can see of the office is holding still. Maybe the world is plummeting like a runaway elevator with me inside. The lights go out. The dark is much more dense than a room where the power has surged. Light seems to have never existed. I am not falling through darkness, but through nothingness, falling so fast I catch up to the future and stop, suspended in what feels like air, then water, then solid matter, but only on my back. I am lying on something soft, a mattress, propped up at the waist. My eyes are closed. I hear voices. They ask me if I am awake. I pretend I am not. Every second I spend in my imaginary sleep is one less second I have to spend on earth.

They wonder if the revival worked, speaking at normal volume, no hint of a hushed tone because they want me to wake up anyway. I know who they are. I recognize the voices of Gina and Jalen. They both sound worried, Gina a little more than Jalen. I am curious if Kelly is part of the scheme.

I consider a sudden scream, jerking forward, eyeballs bulging, unleashing the loudest, longest shriek I can muster. Maybe lock eyes with the first one I see, grab the hand of another. I think it would be funny. But I also think if I start screaming, I may never stop.

When I do open my eyes, rather than look at any of them, I look down to see if my Monterey sweatshirt made it through.

Of course it did not. It was from a place that only existed for me and a friend. I wish I had not thrown the paper at Devin. If I clutched it hard enough, maybe it would have come through with me. It was only a tattered piece of paper ripped from a bag. Those exist here.

They have me dressed in a hospital gown, which makes sense since I am in a hospital room.

"What a relief," Gina is the first to address me. "You had us worried."

"We weren't sure you would make it," Jalen joins in.

"Welcome back, sir," says Kelly.

So she is in on it. I look at her with grave disappointment.

"Some dream, huh?" she tries to deflect my look.

"Yeah," Jalen picks up the thread. "You kept saying something about being a clone."

"You were out so long I imagine you had a lot of crazy dreams," Gina says.

I survey the three of them, plus the two mute people standing behind them, a man and a woman dressed as though they are on the legal team.

"That's your play?" I ask anyone willing to answer.

The three members of Devin's inner circle bat their eyes at each other, while the two suits continue to stare at me.

"What do you mean?" Gina stalls.

"It was all a dream..." I mock the tired out when-in-doubt ending.

"Maybe 'dream' isn't the right word," Jalen grasps for a counterpoint. "Whatever comes to mind in a coma might be classified as something else. Hallucinations?"

"Visions?" Gina pitches in.

"Save your energy," I tell them. "I know what I am."

Gina turns to the buttoned-up twosome.

"Would you excuse us?" she asks them to leave.

They oblige without a word.

"Well," Jalen says when they are gone. "That makes things easier."

"It was worth a shot," Gina makes light of the effort.

"Which might have worked if you hadn't made your little speech to him before he went under," Jalen refuses to play along.

"My little speech never would have crossed my mind if Devin hadn't pulled his little face-to-face stunt."

"You could have kept it to yourself."

"I wanted to make Devin's life more difficult if he ever needed him again."

"What about us?"

"Why would I think we would need him?"

"This was your idea!" he flails his arm in my direction.

"Which I didn't come up with until later!"

"Where do I sign?" I interrupt their sparring.

They stare at me, Kelly included.

"At the bottom of the business purchase agreement, obviously," I capitalize on their attention. "But are we having a public ceremony? Or just going to a lawyer's office? Maybe right here, in the presence of the two stiffs on retainer in the hall."

They look more than scared, as though shown the exact date and manner of their death. Devin might have enjoyed the spectacle, but I find their faces unnerving.

"How do you know?" Gina struggles to say.

"Why would I share any secrets of the universe with you people?"

I am not sure if I am ready to stand, but the timing is perfect, so I make my move and am relieved to encounter no problems with balance.

Once upright, I take the next step, which is taking steps.

"So," I say upon arrival in front of them. "Where are we going?"

Chapter Eleven

The well-dressed woman and man are lawyers, but not for our company. They are from the lab responsible for my creation and storage, and their responsibilities end when I walk out the door of the hospital room ahead of Devin's two-faced trio. I am dressed in the same quarter-zip pullover outfit I was wearing for the launch. It smells clean. At least they washed it.

The lawyers look me over, then turn to leave.

"Is there one person?" I ask them.

They stop and face me.

"One person who built me," I clarify.

"You were a team effort," the woman says.

"Like any program these days," the man adds. "It's too much for one person."

"One person who came up with the idea, then," I follow up.

They look at each other.

"Devin," the woman says. "It was his idea."

"But he didn't know how to make you," the man says.

"That's where the team comes in," the woman repeats the theme.

They nod and turn to finish their retreat.

Devin's team joins me in the hall.

Gina scoffs as we watch them walk away.

"I think that clone company is actually run by clones," she says.

I withhold a response.

Nobody else says anything either the whole way to Devin's house. The distance between the hospital and his house is not long, but filled with traffic and stoplights. The cars behind us drive too fast, the cars in front of us too slow. I could have jet skied with dolphins to my version of Maui in the time it takes to drive a couple of miles.

When Jalen pulls the car into Devin's driveway, we may as well be pulling into another part of the company campus. His house looks like an extension of his office, made of sharp edges and long lines of metal and glass. Wood makes cameo appearances in strategic places, weathered and refinished soft spots revived from long-gone houses that were far more inviting than the one their fragments are now fastened to, old pieces sampled as melodies to lay over the synthetic, thumping beat of the new property.

"The signing is scheduled to start at ten tomorrow morning," Gina says as I stare out the window at the house. "Most of the signatures and initials are already in place. We saved the last few for the ceremony. We'll come pick you up at nine."

"I'd like to look over the contracts," I say while still looking at the house. For all the effort Devin put into its design, it leaves no impression on the mind I inherited from him.

I imagine the silence behind me is not peaceful. They are probably gritting their teeth and glaring at one another.

"The contracts," Gina finally responds. "Sure. I can send you the file, or have someone deliver them to your door."

"I'll just look them over in the morning when we get to the office."

"Oh," she sounds relieved. "Okay."

"I'm only looking for one thing."

"What's that?"

"Sixty-five percent."

I turn to face them. Jalen grips the steering wheel and looks through the windshield as though the car is still in motion. Kelly looks out the window in the backseat behind Jalen, as if pretending to be on the same imaginary drive. Gina is stuck addressing me.

"And you will find that number," she says. "That percentage."

"Good," I smile.

I grip the door handle, then let go and face them again.

"Was it an accident?" I ask.

Jalen and Kelly seem to be driving even faster in their minds. Gina retains her position as spokesperson.

"It started out as one," she sinks into the recollection. "We didn't really plan a takeover. We might have entertained the idea now and then, over drinks after work on Fridays. Then the opportunity presented itself. Devin thought he knew more about scuba diving than he really did."

"Devin thought he knew more about everything than he really did," Jalen adds.

Kelly appreciates the chance to snort a laugh.

"When his oxygen levels started getting dangerous," Gina continues. "We let it play out."

"Wasn't there a guide with you? Or a boat captain?"

"We had Devin," Jalen jumps back in, sarcasm blazing. "Who needs experts? We put his gear back in the boat and told the rental people when we made it back to shore that he got an emergency call so he chartered a sea plane to pick him up right out on the water. They thought that sounded pretty awesome."

"When we got home, we fetched you for the hospital bit," Gina picks up the rest of the story. "The clone company was able to rig it so we could check you in unconscious and claim you had been suffering from fainting spells, that you weren't waking up from this latest episode, and we were all very frightened."

"You pitched it to the cloners as a reset, not a cover-up," I assume.

"They were paid handsomely for their efforts," she confirms my hunch. "They think Devin is still alive, and that he realized introducing himself to you was a terrible mistake."

We sit in silence, probably not in honor of Devin, but certainly thinking of him.

"Since we're sharing secrets..." Kelly assumes she has more of a connection with me than the other two.

Before she can follow through on asking her question, I follow through on escaping from the car.

I keep the door open and lean in to answer her after all, even though she never did ask.

"You'll find out soon enough on your own," I tell her. "Everyone does."

I pronounce the word "does" in quick fashion, so that someone might hear it as "dies" if they want to. I hope at least one of them does.

Devin's house is mine for the taking if I want it.

Treading the lacquered floors reveals what an easy transition it would be. There is nothing personal on the walls or shelves I am not already familiar with. No family members appear in any of the photos, no keepsakes gather dust from before he was hailed. Everything is from his corporate peak. I saunter through another lap around the house, and learn nothing more about him. I already know the people in the pictures. I have memories of receiving the awards now lit by the setting sun sinking through the windows. The house amplifies every footstep I take into an echo louder than anything he left behind.

I am surprised at how tired I am. Being revived is exhausting. I choose a guest bedroom, the one farthest away from the master bedroom, and wonder what to do with this place. I could leave it to a family in need, maybe more than one, but that would rile up the neighbors and draw attention to Devin doing something noble.

Not many people knew him. They only knew his products. Introducing him to the world through the ways I want to live his life would earn him a reputation he does not deserve. Better to sell the house and use the money to build multi-family homes through a charitable company funded by an anonymous donor. Anonymity will be my guiding principle in doing things with his money he never considered.

I start by turning down every interview request Kelly runs by me as she drives us to the office.

"Not even tech media?" she tries to rescue some promises she must have made.

"Nobody," I reiterate. "A good start in disappearing from public life is to not announce that you're disappearing from public life."

"Okay," she surrenders without understanding, turning her attention to the world in motion around us, complaining about traffic, but really about me.

"Gina and Jalen copped out, huh?" I ask when we stop at a red light.

"They'll be there."

"But they left you to be my shepherd."

"There's a lot they need to do to prepare."

"They want to look me in the eye as little as possible."

"You can be a little hard to look at," she acknowledges. "Not physically, but you know, it's kind of like looking into the first moments of the universe, or the last."

"Hmm," I mull how much more of an effect I have on them than I imagined.

"Or a black hole."

"I can see that."

"Or staring into the void, but that sounds cliché. I wanted to come up with something more interesting."

"Okay, I get it."

"Like death puts down his scythe and pulls back his hood—"

"I get it."

The light turns green and she redirects her attention to the road. We are on a street that could pass for a freeway if not for the controlled intersections and manicured landscaping along the center divider.

"Sorry for the dramatic descriptions," she says as we reach cruising speed.

"I understand."

"I know they're not accurate. You're not like that. You just experienced something out of reach, something hard to explain."

The corporate campus looms ahead.

"Aw," I take note of our location.

"What?"

"I was going to explain everything to you, but we're almost there."

She responds to my smug silence with sullen silence.

The corridors of the company are filled with faces I recognize. Some I have met in person, other faces are memories passed down from Devin. Which ones are which, I will never know, since I plan to never see any of them again. I shake any hand extended to me and say little other than "thank you" and "you too". Kelly guides me by the elbow whenever I pause for an exchange that is forgotten as it happens. I am not interested in lingering any more than she is in allowing me to linger, but I appreciate the visual excuse she provides to keep me moving past the doorways and desks of the real and imagined.

Gina and Jalen wave us over into a conference room and they shut door behind us.

"I feel like we made it into the barn before the storm hit," I take a deep breath.

"So are we cows in that scenario?" Kelly plays along.

"I was thinking we corralled the horses."

"So we're cowboys," Jalen beams.

"More like rustlers."

"No," Gina cuts in before Jalen and I can growl at each other. "No, please don't, because we have the contracts here, and as you'll see, they're exactly the same as before the scuba diving incident."

She leads me over to the table where the papers are arranged in pristine piles.

"I need a list of our lawyers who specialize in great big mounds of paper," I say as I make my way to the table.

"You said you were going to look them over yourself," Gina reminds me.

"I am," I sit down before the spread of legalese as if ready to dine on it. "But I'm going to need a lawyer for the kinds of things I want to do after the deal is done."

"Part of the deal is a non-compete clause," she says. "You can't start another company like this one for at least ten years."

"I haven't the slightest interest in starting another company like this one."

"Just as well," Jalen chips in. "You never had any good ideas. All you ever had was a lot of money."

"I think you have me confused with someone else."

He smothers a laugh, which I am proud to have inspired.

I quit while I am ahead and pretend to pore over the contracts. I find what I am looking for within minutes, but keep reading, challenging myself to stay focused when each sentence is like taking a sedative. By the time the buyers arrive, I am convinced the language is ammunition in a war of attrition, each side bidding to lull the other into a blunder.

I never met the buyers, and soon realize Devin never did either. Our relationship has been long-distance, our lawyers playing matchmaker. There are four of them, more or less. It is difficult to tell who are the buyers, who are their lawyers, and who are mine. We joke about going way back as we pose for some pictures, starting with a few action shots of us scribbling our signatures. The lawyers reveal their identities by hovering over us to make sure we sign on the correct lines. Then we shake hands for a photographer. The buyers ask me if I want to join them for lunch to celebrate. I take a deep breath and admit I would rather not, which they think is hilarious.

"I like your honesty!" says one.

"I like saving money on lunch!" says another.

The other one or two of them say nothing. They supply the laugh track and some back slaps. The lawyers for all concerned do less than that. They wait until the first quiet moment to lead the team of buyers out the door, leaving me and my team behind with the photographer for a long, chilly moment that the photographer attempts to warm up.

"How about a picture with the four of you?"

I assume they want to say no with as much volume and emphasis as I do, but they also hold back for some reason as well. My reason is because as fraught as our relationship may be, we have gone through something deep and wide together.

We say nothing and merge into a line. I wonder if Gina or Jalen or Kelly smile. I cannot quite manage one. The photographer gives us no directions, so maybe they are smiling, or maybe the photographer has certain ideas about people in our business, and the way we look fits that point of view.

When the photographer says "thanks" and leaves us, the room is no less tense. We continue to stand in a line as if the photographer is still there. Designed to be a smooth talker, I should be the one to supply the verbal cues that break us up, but have found when choosing my words carefully, I often choose too many of them.

"I'm sorry if I foiled your caper," I decide to say. "But this sale still leaves you with plenty of money to start up whatever you have in mind. Even more than Devin had when he started out."

None of them respond, but our line disperses. They shuffle into different sections of the floor.

"Now if I could have that list of attorneys, and use of the room, I'll be out of your hair by noon."

"We'll be out of here before you," says Jalen. "We've got no hair in this joint anymore."

"You can find the lawyers on the company website," Gina bids me good bye.

Kelly is the only one who tries to end our relationship on a catchy beat. She crosses over and gives me a hug.

"No words," she says.

"That's two," I reply.

"What?" she asks as she undoes herself from me.

"That's two words," I repeat. "If there really are no words, then don't use any."

"Arrogant to the end," Jalen sneers from his part of the room.

"Duplicitous from the beginning," I crack back.

The three of them walk out. Kelly lets herself out last, and mouths to me that she thought what I said was funny, but leaves nonetheless.

They dislike Devin and fear me, so I understand.

I sit at the table now emptied of contracts and scroll through the list of lawyers on my phone. Each entry has their photograph as well as their name and a brief biography. I highlight those with experience in foundations and corporate philanthropy. I disregard all familiar names, faces, and information. I want someone who has not spent any time with Devin, who went to the least impressive law school, whose name I cannot recall, someone who is content to do their job unbeknownst to anyone who could do them any favors.

Six of them meet my minimum qualifications. I bring the candidates in for interviews to see who performs the worst. Our sessions are brief. I ask each of them two questions: how they feel about the company being sold, and if they feel any loyalty toward me. If they respond with even a trace of diplomacy or grace, I thank them for coming in and dismiss them. If they stammer all over themselves, I ask more questions to make sure they do not warm up, that they really are as awkward as their first impression.

I narrow it down to two men who look like they might hyperventilate by the fifth question. I invite them to a second interview over lunch at a flirtatious restaurant full of natural light where we used to entertain investors, and I have the two men sit next to each other. I first ask them if this is their kind of place, and then to describe their typical weekend.

They both nail the question about whether this is their kind of place. Candidate One makes a face and says maybe for a special occasion. Candidate Two has an even stronger response. He says nothing. All he does is squirm, make a squeaky noise, then shrug.

With regard to the second question, a typical weekend for Candidate One consists of organizing murder mystery parties, which concerns me, because it indicates a higher degree of sociability than I would prefer, but he clarifies that the story designs are a side gig, and he does not actually attend the parties, so I keep him in the running.

Candidate Two once again comes back strong with a long, strained pause.

"I eat," he divulges.

"Anything in particular?" I follow up.

He considers his response.

"A burrito," he says. "Maybe a sandwich."

"And do you do anything before or after you eat? Maybe during?"

"Watch a show?" he seems unsure.

"Is there a certain genre you like? A specific show?"

"Whatever Netflix recommends."

I try to contain my glee at his brilliant answer. He is the undisputed leader heading into the final round, which consists of seeing which one of them is the first to say something as we wait for our food.

They both keep quiet, as if they somehow know what I have in mind. Maybe I failed to sufficiently disguise my delight when Candidate Two crushed the weekend question.

When we start to eat, Candidate One remarks that his food tastes good.

The search is over.

When he is done eating, I thank him for coming and ask if I may have a word with Candidate Two, who is still picking at his food. Candidate One obliges, perhaps thinking he won the job over Candidate Two, who is also under that impression.

"Did I do something wrong?" Candidate Two asks.

"No," I assure him. "You got the job if you want it."

He is surprised. I wonder if this is too much to handle for a man not used to good news.

"Do you have a health care plan?" he asks.

"If you go to a doctor or a hospital, send me the bill."

"I have some pre-existing conditions."

"Like what?"

"Really just one, but it causes all the others."

"Anxiety?"

"How do you know?"

"Lucky guess."

"Is that going to be a problem?"

"I'd like to double what I used to pay you to work for the company," I answer.

"So it's not a problem."

"Is twice as much money and free healthcare a problem?"

He appears on the verge of fainting.

"Stay with me," I half kid.

"Okay," he floats back to earth on a few deep breaths.

"We're going to do some great things," I say in an effort to inspire him.

Instead he starts to fade again, so I clarify the flow chart: I do the great things on my own, then send him the details and directions to draw up contracts when necessary to make the great things official.

"Not all that different from what you're doing now," I summarize, which he seems to think is the best part. He orders a brownie sundae for dessert. I try not to watch him eat it as I finish the water in my glass.

I see Candidate One looking through the front window, cupping his hands around his face to see us better. I hold up my hands in an apology. Candidate Two catches me doing that in between bites of his brownie and appears ready to panic again.

"That wasn't meant for you," I tell him. "Don't worry."

He eases back into his sundae.

Candidate One peels himself off the window and drifts out of frame.

"Great things," I remind my new hire. "Great things."

Chapter Twelve

The first great thing involves paying a visit to Phil's parents.

The Dedmons live in a house that appears to have been standing since before companies like ours moved into the valley, pumping so much value into the plots of land that the old homes perched on them are swatted away by bulldozers to make way for vain, frosty pseudo-mansions that ooze to the edges of each lot, built by the new owners to justify paying twenty-five times what the original owners put down.

I ring the doorbell, but hear no sound on the other side. Before I can knock, the door opens.

"Mrs. Dedmon?" I ask.

His mother looks about the same age Phil appeared to be during our time together, but age in the afterlife is fluid. He may have wanted to come across as older there, in anticipation of the generation of people he would be hanging out with.

She wears a grey cardigan sweater that reaches her knees. She clenches it up tight, as if to offset opening the door.

"We're not interested in selling," she answers.

"I'm not here about your house, Mrs. Dedmon."

The gravity of what I am about to tell her pulls me with more force than I expected. I was too excited about my plan to think about how I might introduce it. With that in mind, I decide the best option is to get to the plan as soon as possible.

"I'm here about your son."

Her face pales and lengthens.

"My son is dead."

As soon as possible comes too soon.

"I know," I backtrack. "I'm sorry. I knew him."

"Really?" she says, and there is a faint note of joy in her reaction.

"He worked at my company for a while."

"Oh," she is disappointed. "You weren't friends?"

I want to tell her everything, deliver the news that may free her from long sweaters and long days. Your son, I want to say to her, may not have had many friends in this life, but wait until you see him in the next life. His friendship is one of the best parts.

The door opens wider, revealing Mr. Dedmon, who looks a lot like Phil. They even look the same age, building on my freshly-minted case that Phil went with an older look in the afterlife.

"You're the video game guy," he sounds somewhat accusatory.

"Yes," I try to answer with enough brightness to fend off his negativity, but not so much as to disrespect the moment.

"Devin Orr," he recalls.

"That's right," I confirm.

"It's not a hard question," he returns to what his wife asked while he was still behind the door. "Were you friends with Phil or not?"

"Yes," I tell them.

"He never mentioned being friends with the head of the company," his father presses me. "That seems like the kind of thing that might mean a lot to a guy from the maintenance department."

"Your average guy, maybe," I say. "But your son was a humble, decent man not prone to bragging."

He goes from grilling me to not being able to speak.

"Would you like to come in?" Mrs. Dedmon takes over and steps aside.

I express my gratitude and follow them into their living room. We sit in couches on opposite sides of a coffee table.

After I decline Mrs. Dedmon's beverage offer, Mr. Dedmon regains his footing.

"Why weren't you at his service?" he asks.

"It's one of my biggest regrets. And I have a lot of regrets."

"We could have used a few more people," he says, which wounds his wife.

"I'd like to make it up to you," I tell them both while concentrating on her. "And to him, to Phil, if I may."

They wait in wonder for what I have in mind.

I have made it to the plan. I inhale satisfaction, and exhale relief.

"I sold the company recently, and in addition to a lot of money, it also led to a lot of reassessment and reflection. More than anything else, I find myself dwelling on how many people I relied on who just did their jobs with no fanfare and no fawning. Your son was the ultimate example of that."

Mrs. Dedmon grasps her husband's hand. They look at each other. I hold on until they look ready to continue.

"I would like to start a foundation in his name."

They look at each other again, their glow of anticipation giving way to a touch of confusion.

"That sounds very nice," Mr. Dedmon speaks on their behalf, looking at his wife during the compliment before turning to me for the question. "But what exactly is a foundation?"

"We've heard the word before," Mrs. Dedmon says. "It's one of those things you think you know about until you actually have to know about it."

"Well," I aim for the center of all the definitions swirling around in my head, "it's an account used for charity, that builds on its investments, so it's ongoing. You can use it to fund all sorts of different projects, or it can focus on one particular goal. It can take the form of scholarships, donations, buildings, you name it."

Their glow returns in the form of recognition.

"And I mean it when I say you name it," I seize the phrase I have provided myself. "Whatever project you want, name it, then we can come up with an amount for the initial investment and a plan to keep it viable."

They each react like my lawyer did when I outlined his terms of employment.

"You don't have to tell me now," I ease up. "I'll leave my card and you can take your time. When you have an idea, let me know and my attorney will start working on the details."

I put my card on the table between us.

"If I don't hear from you, you'll hear from me," I get up to leave. "I know that sounds annoying, and it is. That's the whole idea. It's motivation."

"I've got it," Mrs. Dedmon declares.

I sit back down and look at her with almost as much curiosity as her husband does.

She loosens her cardigan and lowers it off her shoulders, revealing the spaghetti straps of her nightgown.

"I'm not trying to be sexy," she explains. "I can't have anything on my shoulders for long."

"What do you think the foundation should cover, dear," Mr. Dedmon encourages her to stay on topic.

"It starts to press down on me," she further clarifies her off-the-shoulder look for my sake.

Curiosity seems to be the best reaction. It can apply to her condition, and what she has in mind for her son's legacy, so I nod with curiosity.

Her shoulders free and loose, she launches into her pitch.

"Phil struggled in school," she says. "He had an Individual Education Plan, but there was only so much they could do. He needed extra help. Private tutoring was expensive. We took out a loan on the house so we could afford it. He finally caught up to grade level after three years of one-on-one work with a tutor."

The more I learn about Phil, the more I like him.

"I was so grateful we could do that for him," she proceeds. "And I always wondered what it would feel like if we couldn't. What it would feel like to watch your child struggle and not be able to do enough about it, to watch him get worse, get more angry, hate school more every year. What it would be like to watch his life be so hard before it should be. If we didn't have this house, what would we have done?"

She is asking a rhetorical question, but Mr. Dedmon looks at the ground as if looking for an answer.

"I want to make sure kids who need that kind of help can get it," she announces.

I join Mr. Dedmon in gazing at the ground.

"Well," I let my gratitude flow over meeting them before I look up. "Let's make that happen."

We spend some time batting around ideas.

She is less concerned with promoting the program and more concerned with making sure the most deserving kids and their families are introduced to it. She would like it promoted to counselors, who could then identify strong candidates through their office visits and teacher recommendations. The money would not only fund scholarships for the students, but pay to upgrade tutoring services in towns where demand starts to swell thanks to the program.

When the subject turns to getting my lawyer involved to make the Philip Dedmon Foundation official, I slide in an additional detail.

"He's also going to draft a nondisclosure agreement for you to sign."

"A nondisclosure agreement?" she cannot help but wonder. "For what?"

"Regarding the identity of your benefactor," I put it formally before putting it simply. "Me."

Mrs. Dedmon has stolen the show since we started discussing her vision, so when they both look perplexed over my request, Mr. Dedmon resurfaces to deliver a line.

"Aren't those for bad things?" he asks. "Things people want to cover up?"

"Anonymity is very important to me in this new phase of my life. Most anonymous donors secretly hope they get discovered, but I'm serious. No one can know my name. If that happens, I pull the money."

They look taken aback, but not concerned.

"Your secret is safe with us," Mrs. Dedmon raises her hand as though being sworn in.

"Scout's honor," Mr. Dedmon adds his hand to the air above them.

"Do people still say that?" his wife teases him.

"I'm not sure if I ever said it before," he realizes.

"You're bringing it back," I cheer their turn toward weightlessness.

They glance at one another for a second that carries decades of shared history.

I put my hands on my knees to signal I am about to rise from the couch.

"Before you go," Mrs. Dedmon reads my sign. "Do you have any stories about Phil you could tell us?"

I was so close.

"Huh," I hedge. "Let me see..."

There was that time we jet skied with dolphins to a seaside city he created.

"I don't mean to put you on the spot," she apologizes. "It's just that our conversations with you and your lawyer are going to be so legal and official, and when the foundation gets going, everything will be about his name, not about him."

"That's true," I say, hoping my response is appropriate, because I am too busy trying to come up with a story rather than listen to the reason why she wants it.

Instead of composing an original, I happen upon one of the memories Phil shared about Devin and borrow it as my source material.

"I had some of those string lights over the patio outside my office," I tell them. "I loved to sit out there and think about things after everyone had gone home, how the latest project was going, what our next move should be. When one of the lights burnt out and Phil replaced it, he noticed the glow was a little different from the rest. I told him it didn't matter, but he insisted on replacing every bulb from the same supply so the lights would shine the same. 'That one light might distract you,' he said. I thought it was silly at first. I mean, that's all it would take to distract me? What am I, a moth? Then I realized, after he replaced them all, he was right. Maybe I was reading more into the glow than was really there, but it felt right. After he left to work for the city, I thought about him whenever I looked at those lights. A lot of people did things for me, but only because they wanted something. Phil is the only person I can think of at my company who did something out of concern and goodness, not selfishness."

The looks on the faces of the Dedmons make me feel as though we are sitting around a campfire rather than a coffee table.

"The next time one of those bulbs burnt out," I find a way to lower the curtain on my version of events. "I replaced it myself, and was glad to see it had a different shine. Nobody noticed. Nobody offered to fix the situation. Nobody would probably think of it as a situation that needed fixing. And that was fine by me. I had no interest in changing the rest of the bulbs. I let that light glow on its own terms for as long as it shined. Nobody was like your son."

They appear to be watching the embers of the imaginary fire die down.

I finally follow through on rising from the couch.

Mrs. Dedmon hoists the cardigan back up over her shoulders and maneuvers her way around the coffee table with her hand extended, "If I can't thank you in public, then I thank you a million times right now and forever."

I shake her hand.

"If I was comfortable hugging people," she says. "I would do that too."

"This is one of my top five all-time handshakes," I assure her as it comes to a close.

Mr. Dedmon and I nod and wave to each other from across the coffee table as I head for the doorway.

"Here, let me..." Mrs. Dedmon reaches the door before I do and opens it.

Before I pass through, she grabs my arm, gathers whatever courage she can muster, and gives me a hug.

Mr. Dedmon looks proud of his wife, the kind of pride he must have felt whenever Phil did something that made him beam, like graduate high school after all that hard work, become good at his job, build a career, and make his mother even more proud, and beam even brighter than his father.

Their lights continue to shine on me as I make my way to the next stop.

They flicker a bit as I have to concentrate on driving more than Devin would.

I have memories of driving, but no experience. During my first time on earth, I was always a passenger, shuttled around to the various meetings and presentations so we could prepare and debrief in the backseat to avoid any wasted motion. I find heavy traffic makes me a better driver, as the swarm of cars forces me to concentrate and conjures up embedded instincts, while the open road allows me to grow complacent and reflect on the Dedmons' rays.

The parking lot I pull into is surrounded by the artwork Jane told me about, the wooden boards as big as dining room tabletops swirling with images of whatever each kid felt like painting that day during the art festival that year.

I climb out of the car and feel as though I have stumbled upon a lost city, a legend handed down for generations at long last discovered. The displays are perched on their posts like totems. As I walk toward the address of Jane's widower and children, I check the date on each wooden canvas I pass to see if one of them marks the year that contains the notorious mouse painted by Jane's determined daughter. Before I can discover the sacred artifact, I arrive at the residence of the artist.

They live in an apartment building I may have passed by five hundred times and never noticed. While the Dedmon house still stands because they refuse to sell, I suspect these apartments still stand because the law requires a certain number of rental units in a tight market like this town, and not enough money can be made in building new ones that are as affordable.

I climb the exterior staircase that leads to their unit on the second floor. When Jane's husband answers the door, he studies me as if I am a quiz question.

"Huh," he says in the same way he might respond to his youngest daughter if she suddenly decided to tell him that Little Rock is the capitol of Arkansas for no particular reason.

"Hello, sir," I say. "I'm—"

"I know who you are."

"Oh?"

"Well done."

"Thank you."

"Fainting spells shouldn't be ignored, especially in someone your age."

"Oh. I thought you meant—"

"That, too. Pretty penny you got for it."

"You really stay up to date on the industry news."

"I guess it was a good time to get out. Most people who suffer from fainting spells are less than half your age. It's a young person's condition."

"So is our industry," I lay out a path toward a lighter tone.

He does not follow it.

"We take our health for granted," he maintains. "Without it, we're nothing."

I feel as though he is providing an opportunity to offer condolences for Jane, but as I try to scribble a line in my head and deliver it, he cuts me off with a line of his own.

"Thank you for stopping by before you grew a beard and found the perfect stick to use as a staff."

I get defensive, which requires no rough drafts or rehearsals.

"I didn't make any announcements."

"But that's what you're doing, right?" he seems to have prepared for a confrontation with me. "Giving away a bunch of money to get that line to creep up the y-axis of good deeds since you've spent all your time on the x-axis of character being a selfish bore."

I take a deep breath. I suspected this was possible.

"The family of a former employee started a scholarship fund," I roll out the alternate pitch.

"I'm already putting money into a 529 plan."

"Not for college," I enthuse. "For kids who need tutoring so they can maybe go to college someday."

"What makes you think either of our girls needs tutoring?"

"I don't know if they do. But when that family came to me and wanted help starting this foundation, I thought it was a fantastic idea and wanted to share it with someone right away who might benefit, but I don't know anyone with kids."

"No one?"

"Well," I admit. "Nobody with kids that I like."

He backs off and slows down.

"Are you saying you don't like the people who have the kids?" he asks. "Or you don't like the kids."

"I'd say it's about 75 percent parents, 25 percent kids."

He grins.

A little girl appears from behind his hip.

"Hello," I greet her.

Her father is surprised to find her there.

"Hello," she replies. "Who are you?"

"A salesman," her father says before I can answer.

"What are you selling?" she asks.

"Tutoring," I answer. "Extra help for school."

"My big sister needs that."

"Huh," I take my turn using that same term in the same tone in which her father greeted me.

"Speaking of your big sister," her father reaches for a way to end the conversation. "Why don't you go in and see if she has any ideas about dinner."

"Okay," she complies. "Good bye, salesman."

"Good bye," I wave as she vanishes back into the apartment.

Her father and I shift our weight back and forth and exchange brief, sheepish glances in honor of the uncomfortable moment his daughter created.

"I'll take a card, or a brochure," he says. "Whatever you have."

I hand him a card.

"We don't have brochures yet."

"Too soon," he accepts the card.

"Too soon," I echo.

He looks at the card longer than necessary, using it as a tiny paper shield to protect whatever he wants to keep hidden.

"Did your girls contribute to any of those wonderful works of art around the parking lots?" I ask.

"Yes," he comes out from behind the card, perhaps too soon for his liking. Everything in his life of late must seem to be too soon.

"Which ones?" I follow up. "Where are they?"

"Our oldest has some doodles on a couple over in the parking lot by the Italian restaurant, back before our youngest was able to get in on it. Then they're both on a few more in the lot behind the bakery."

I hold out my hand.

He accepts it.

"I hope you decide to give us a try," I tell him. "This is much bigger than me."

No doubt he will never use my name for any reason, so I hold off on my request for anonymity and leave our conversation where it is.

I walk to the bakery and pass through it on my way to the parking lot I seek. They have one loaf of bread left following the morning and early afternoon rush. I buy it and take the bag with me out back in search of a certain work of art.

I find it facing a large SUV with two children's car seats visible through the back window, as if the vehicle is pointing me in the right direction. I locate the painting of something with large ears and a long tail, purported to be a mouse, which is in fact the most meticulous rendering of anything featured on the wooden slab.

I imagine the wood laid out on the ground in the park on that day Jane is re-creating in the afterlife yet again, her latest redo of that day in a line so long she has lost track of what number she is on. I picture her lingering nearby her oldest daughter, trying not to hover as she watches her child struggle with what she wants to portray. Meanwhile the younger daughter finishes her drawing, whichever one it is, within seconds and runs to the next activity, or to the fountain. I look at the whole piece, all the little paintings on it, and try to imagine the crowd of kids responsible for them. I wonder how close Jane comes to including them in her simulation with any accuracy, or if they are all just background noises and shapes, nameless and faceless points in time plotted on water, rippling away, played by random projections in her retelling of the story. I reach into the bag and feed off the loaf of bread, tearing off chunks as I scan every contribution to the work, the paint on the wood, the moments dried, faded, and cracking. My focus softens and the individual drawings blend into a whole, a whirl of shifting colors that sometimes seems far away, other times closer, depending on how big a bite of bread I am chewing and the kaleidoscope my labor creates.

Having connected with the two contacts I wanted to help, I ponder what to do next and where to go.

For the what to do next, finding people who need a financial boost is easy enough. Daily scans of the news and crowdfunding sites takes care of how to spend the money.

The where to go is more complicated. I could avoid having a fixed address and drive around, now that I am getting used to driving, with nothing but a post office box as my headquarters. If I settle on a permanent address, I would prefer a small, nondescript apartment in a town far from the valley, someplace filled with people who were born in that town and people who ended up there out of necessity, not by choice. I want nothing to do with a cabin in the country. Every early retiree from tech seems to go that route, for at least one of their houses. No need to work that hard to avoid the public eye. Nobody outside the valley will recognize me. I need to get to know people, not turn my back on them.

I already feel more human by not knowing what happens after this life reaches its limit. I hold out hope that I may be allowed back into the hereafter as I am, adventures intact. Devin and I would never cross paths, unless we decide to meet once in a while and insult each other, which fulfills the afterlife directive because we would both enjoy it. He will never spend any time with anyone I miss, he said as much, and I have plenty of excuses in mind I could offer my old friends, a different one for each person, to explain my absence and pick up where we left off. Maybe management would allow me to tell everyone I love the truth.

If they let me in.

The uncertainty helps remind me that giving away as much money as I can is about what happens here, and has nothing to do with what comes next. All I want to know is whether I get to remember any of it. But I have a feeling this is my only chance to be this person.

I take another bite of bread, take a long look at the drawings from the past, and vow to take advantage of the unknown.

Also by Sean Boling

The Current Mr. Orr
Devin's Best Afterlife
Once in Two Lifetimes
Revenge and Wellness in the Sweet Hereafter

Standalone
Cut Flowers
Abraham the Anchor Baby Terrorist
The Summer of Our Foreclosure
Satellite Campus
A Charter to That Other Place
The Latest Version of My Love Story
Show Them What They Won
The Name Field
Should
Moral Adjacent
Over Here We Have
The Current Mr. Orr

About the Author

Sean lives with his family in Templeton, California. He teaches English at Cuesta College.

www.ingramcontent.com/pod-product-compliance
Lightning Source LLC
Chambersburg PA
CBHW051451130726
47987CB00005B/2260